Sand-Catcher

Sand-Catcher

Omar Khalifah

translated by Barbara Romaine

COFFEE HOUSE PRESS
Minneapolis
2024

Coffee House Press books are available to the trade through our primary distributor, Consortium Book Sales & Distribution, cbsd.com or (800) 283-3572. For personal orders, catalogs, or other information, write to info@coffeehouse press.org.

Coffee House Press is a nonprofit literary publishing house. Support from private foundations, corporate giving programs, government programs, and generous individuals helps make the publication of our books possible. We gratefully acknowledge their support in detail in the back of this book.

LIBRARY OF CONGRESS CATALOGING-IN-PUBLICATION DATA

Names: Khalifah, Omar, 1980 – author | Romaine, Barbara, 1959 – translator.
Title: Sand-Catcher. English
Description: First English language edition. | Minneapolis; Coffee House Press,
    2024
Identifiers: LCCN: 2024940385 (print)
ISBN: 9781566897334 (paperback) | ISBN 9781566897341 (epub)

PRINTED IN THE UNITED STATES OF AMERICA

32 31 30 29 28 27 26 25   1 2 3 4 5 6 7 8

Translator's Note

I offer here a few words of elucidation as to certain features of this novel. The first of these concerns an unusual challenge I found myself called upon to address as the translator: I had to decide what to do about the names of the major characters, for the simple reason that they are given none. For about half of them it was possible simply to use an English rendition of the verbal descriptions applied to them: "the grandfather," "the grandson," and so on. The four journalists around whom most of the action is centered, however, are another matter. One is identified as "the leader," another "the translator," and I could have used these terms, except that the other two journalists—a man and a woman who are both unfaithful to their spouses—are assigned a single identifying word that alludes to their marital treachery. A gender marker consistent with Arabic grammar and orthography differentiates the woman from the man, so the closest English equivalents would be "adulterer" and "adultress"—which are accurate but ponderously biblical. In the end I decided simply to transliterate the designations of each of the four journalists and refer to them by these transliterations as if the words were in fact their names: hence "Qaa'id," for "leader" and "Mutarjima" for "translator," with "Khaa'in" and "Khaa'ina" identifying the adulterer and the adulteress, respectively.

An additional point perhaps calling for explanation is that, in a scene about halfway through the novel, characters are found in attendance at their white-collar jobs on a Sunday; this is because, in most Arab countries, Sunday is typically a work day, Friday being the day of worship for the majority of the population.

Finally, for help with a selection of non-English terms, here is a brief alphabetical glossary:

'ammi: "my uncle," this term is commonly used to address an elder with respect.

arghilah (regional variations include *narghilah, hookah,* and *shisha*): a device for smoking tobacco (or sometimes hashish) consisting of a flexible or bamboo pipe attached to a bottle-like receptacle filled with water, through which smoke is drawn to filter and cool it.

hijab: any of various styles of headscarf worn by some Muslim women to cover not the face but the head and usually the neck as well; the more conservative *niqab* covers all of the face except for the eyes, in addition to the head and neck.

kufiyyah: a type of check-patterned cotton scarf worn in some Middle Eastern societies, usually by men, on the head or around the neck; varieties of *kufiyyah* are distinguished by colors and patterns that may indicate tribal or regional affiliation. In the context of Palestine, the *kufiyyah* has become a symbol of the Palestinian aspiration for liberation and self-determination.

maqlouba: a traditional Palestinian rice-based dish featuring meat, vegetables, and various spices, prepared in a pot that is inverted onto a plate before the meal is served; the word *maqlouba* means, literally, "upside-down."

mukhtar: village chief

Nakba: catastrophe; used as a proper noun to refer to the war of 1948—when the state of Israel was founded—in the course of which hundreds of thousands of Palestinians were either driven into exile or massacred outright.

Naksa: setback; used as a proper noun for the six-day war of June 1967, which culminated in Israel's occupation of the West Bank, Gaza, the Sinai Peninsula, and the Golan Heights.

Sand-Catcher

I

The Interview

WE ENTERED THE APARTMENT PEACEABLY ENOUGH. We had digital recorders, papers, smart tablets, cameras, and nineteen questions. The previous night, we had gathered at Turtle Green Café on Rainbow Street in Amman: my friend who was cheating on his wife, my friend who was cheating on her husband, another friend fluent in three languages, and I. We sat for a long time thinking about what sort of questions we should ask the old man. It had taken us weeks to get the family to agree to meet with us, for one reason and another—the old man was sick, say, or they were too busy. He had this hothead of a grandson who yelled at us every time we called, refusing even to hear us out. At one point, Khaa'in (my friend who was cheating on his wife), on the phone with me as he headed for a rendezvous with his girlfriend, suggested we just forget the whole thing. Then we could turn our attention to some other newsworthy topic to report on. But I had concluded that the interview with the old man was important—essential, even. To most of us it was a matter of principle, so it was worth taking some trouble over. Our meeting at the café lasted three hours, and everyone agreed that I should be the one to speak for the group when dealing with the old man. I didn't quite get why they chose me, but I agreed. "Al-qaa'id"—the Leader—they called me, laughing. We wrote down ten questions to start with, as well as five alternates (in case the old man had trouble answering some of the original ten), plus—just in case—three more we weren't sure would fly, and finally one concluding question we thought we might ask, "depending on how things go," as Khaa'ina (my friend who was cheating on her husband) put it. We agreed that Mutarjima (my friend who is fluent in three languages) would record the interview, so that we could transcribe and edit it later. I asked Khaa'in and Khaa'ina to turn off their cell phones during the interview, to avoid interruptions. Khaa'in would take some pictures while Khaa'ina took notes on her tablet, and I would be in charge of our documents—our questions in hard copy, that is.

It had all started a month earlier, when Khaa'in called and told me about a birthday party to be held by his girlfriend's relatives, in honor of a family member who was turning eighty-five.

"So is she going to invite you to the party?"

"Don't be ridiculous. Here's the story. The old man is the last living member of the family who was an eyewitness to the *Nakba*."

"And what's that got to do with me?"

"Think about it, man. The last survivor of the *Nakba* in this family, the only one with actual memories of the events. It's an amazing story."

"How is he related to your girlfriend?"

"He's her grandfather's brother."

So I put the idea to the editor-in-chief of the newspaper we worked for, and he was quite enthusiastic. For the assignment, he chose me, Khaa'in, Khaa'ina, and Mutarjima, giving us absolute autonomy as to the manner of its completion and the format of the interview. The four of us met and speculated about the reason we'd been assigned to the project. The first thing that occurred to all of us was that we were the only ones of Palestinian descent at the paper—no doubt the boss assumed we all harbored our own stories of the *Nakba,* stories we'd heard from our grandparents and other family elders. Perhaps, too, it was because the boss knew we were all friends. And maybe because Khaa'in was the one who had pitched the idea in the first place.

For our first meeting after we'd been assigned to the project, when we went out for coffee, Khaa'ina surprised us by saying, "Name one specific thing, something distinctive, about your connection to Palestine."

Although I couldn't decide whether her suggestion was serious or facetious, I spoke up first, and the others followed suit.

Qaa'id: "I still mix up the colors of the Palestinian flag."

Khaa'in: "All the women I've slept with were Palestinian, except for my wife."

Khaa'ina: "Twenty minutes into my wedding I discovered that we'd set the date for the anniversary of the *Nakba*."

Mutarjima: "The first time in my life that I ever made *maqlouba*, it burned to a crisp, and I threw it in the trash."

As journalists, we weren't experts on Palestine, so we had to do our homework and consult a good many sources in various languages, not only Arabic. The point of the interview was to publish a report on the old man based on his account of his life before and after the *Nakba*. Among the topics our questions covered, we were particularly interested in the moment when he and his family were driven out of Palestine, and when his village fell to the Jews, as well as in the massacres perpetrated by the Zionists. Khaa'ina told me about a novel by a Lebanese writer, *Gate of the Sun,* which featured many tales of the *Nakba*. She thought I should read it so I could refer to some of the issues it raised as I directed our questions to the old man.

I asked Khaa'in to get us the phone number of a member of the subject's family; his girlfriend gave him the grandson's number. We called him from the newspaper offices and told him about our plan. His refusal was startling and absolute; when I asked him for a reason, he hung up on me. We called him back repeatedly, but the young man just yelled at us every time, demanding that we stop bothering him. Khaa'in suggested we talk to his girlfriend and ask for her help with her relatives, but, two days later, he told us that, while she believed in the merits of our project, she didn't think the family would agree to it. When we asked her why, she told us that the old man was very ill, that the subject might be too sensitive for him, and that it might be best not to reopen old wounds. I asked her to try to convince the family that our goal was to safeguard the collective memory of the Palestinian people, considering how few remained of the generation who'd witnessed the *Nakba*. At this, my friends looked at me, impressed, murmuring, "Gate of the Sun." After at least three weeks' worth of back-and-forth, the family agreed— their spokesperson was the old man's eldest son—but with the stipulation that they be allowed to approve the final copy of the report before it went to press.

So we entered the apartment peaceably. The old man was in the center of the room where guests were received, seated on a chair draped in a soft sheepskin, in the midst of a great many family members. For a moment, we felt as if we really were important journalists. The eldest son offered us tea and pastries, and we began by chatting in a general way with the assembled group about our work and our lives. Khaa'in engaged least in the general conversation, and I noticed him staring at one of the young women of the family. After a while the chatter died down; we could tell by the way the family was looking at us that it was time to get on with the business we'd come for. The four of us seated ourselves in front of the old man and introduced ourselves to him, explaining who we were and why we were there. As agreed, I led the discussion.

"My colleagues and I would be so pleased to sit with you and listen to any stories you may be willing to share with us regarding your recollections of the *Nakba*. So as not to take up too much of your time, we've prepared a few questions, which we hope you won't mind answering."

Mutarjima readied her recording equipment, Khaa'in brought out his camera, and Khaa'ina switched on her tablet.

"We have ten questions. We thought we'd divide them into sets, start with the first one, and work our way down the list. This way you can begin by answering whichever question you like from each set."

We looked at the old man, trying to gauge his reaction to this introduction, but his face was expressionless.

"There are three questions in the first set:

1. What is the primary factor that induced you to leave your village in Palestine? Was it the news of the massacres occurring in other villages? Did you hear, for instance, of the massacre at Deir Yassine before or after you left your village?

2. As we understand it, you were fifteen years old at the time of the *Nakba*. Do you recall what relations with the Jews were like before the *Nakba*? Did you mingle with them? When you talked about the Jews, what did you say?

3. Describe for us the moment in which you were driven out, insofar as you remember it. What did you take with you? Where did you go?"

At this point I stopped, and studied the old man's face, as well as those of my colleagues. I believe I acquitted myself well, but I discerned nothing in the old man's features to suggest that he had taken in a single word I said. Smiling, his eldest son tried to lighten the atmosphere, suggesting that we take the conversation in a different direction, but we kept waiting for any sign from the old man. His combative grandson came over and hissed in my ear that we would have to end the proceedings and drop the whole project if the old man didn't speak up within the next minute or two. To get him out of my face, I signaled reluctant agreement, but in my mind I was resolutely determined to hear what the old man had to say. Mutarjima then spoke up, proposing that I move on to the second set of questions. I was concerned that I might inadvertently break up the party—the old man and all his relatives—by asking too many questions, but her suggestion seemed to offer the best way out of the embarrassing silence that had settled over the room.

"What do you say we just go ahead with the second set of questions, *'ammi?* There are three questions in this set as well, and you can answer all of them if you wish, or pick and choose as you like. I can also repeat the questions in the first set, if that would be helpful. Here we go:

4. What happened during the expulsion of the residents of your village? Did you encounter the Jews? Did the village suffer any casualties?

5. Were there any conflicts or disputes among the villagers during the course of the expulsion? Who gave the instructions or orders? Who organized the expulsion?

6. We've heard that there were Palestinians who brought some of their animals with them out of their villages. Could you describe this for us?"

There was no change at all, as if nothing had happened. The same deathly silence, the same chill in the atmosphere. The grandson gave me a look that said this was going nowhere. The eldest son asked me if I wanted to continue. It occurred to me to bypass the third set of questions and skip straight to the end: the question we had prepared as a last resort. We had put a considerable amount of time into crafting something that would be simultaneously provocative and sympathetic. Khaa'in signaled me with a wink, as if he had read my mind. I had written the final question on a slip of paper and stowed it in the inside pocket of my suit jacket. Now I pulled it out.

"There's no pressure to answer these questions immediately, *'ammi.* We can arrange another visit if you wish. We simply wanted to give you a sense of the kind of thing we're looking for. There's one final question my colleagues and I thought of as a means of wrapping up the interview we hope to publish with your help. I hope you will think carefully about it, *'ammi*. You can't imagine how valuable your testimony to the events of the *Nakba* will be. The world has declared war on the collective memory of the Palestinians, *'ammi*, and you're a soldier on the right side of this war. All of us have a duty to tell the world our stories, so that . . ."

"*Get the hell out of here, you motherfuckers!*"

The Grandson

THIS WAS THE LAST THING MY GRANDFATHER NEEDED at the end of his life. When Abir called and told me about the reporters who wanted to set up an interview, I refused, absolutely. I told her we were in the middle of organizing a birthday party for our grandfather, an occasion not at all suitable for that sort of journalistic enterprise. Abir tried again, but I still said no. She was puzzled by my refusal. She cited the dozens of documentaries—not to mention interviews broadcast on radio, television, and so forth—that had been conducted with Palestinians who'd witnessed the *Nakba,* all for the purpose of preserving evidence of the crimes perpetrated by Israel. I just shook my head; I didn't go into the real reason behind my resolve. I told her my grandfather was too easily tired-out to handle a lot of intense discussion. She suggested I let her give my phone number to one of the reporters on the project. I was hesitant at first, but I did want to have my position on record with these people, so I allowed Abir to tell them how to contact me. Two nights later, my phone rang, a number I didn't recognize.

"Hello."

"Hello."

"We're the team of journalists Abir told you about."

"Right. Now listen here, if you try to call me again, I'll find you and shove my phone up your asses, one by one."

I hung up. I thought that would be the end of it, considering the insult, but to my surprise the phone rang again. I picked up the call and shouted into my phone that they'd better leave us alone and mind their own business, but their spokesman—I didn't know his name—took the wind right out of my sails, simply by asking why. What was behind my refusal to allow an interview with my grandfather? I repeated the same arguments I had given Abir, but the reporter was undeterred, and began playing on my refusal as if it was a betrayal of Palestine itself. He reminded me of the importance of this interview, of its moral dimension. I was on the point of taking my refusal to a whole other level, when a thought occurred to me. Why not let them come, after all? Let them just try it. Wouldn't that be the ideal way of teaching these assholes a lesson? I hung up the phone on them again, certain now that they weren't going to give up. Two days later, I got together with Abir. Although I blamed her for this fix she'd got us all into, I went ahead and urged her to make her case to my father—maybe he would agree to let the interview happen.

So it was agreed: the journalists would come to our house three days after my grandfather's birthday party. My father charged me with getting the old man dressed and ready. I woke him up in the morning, made him his breakfast, and we ate. I sat him in front of the television in the living room and turned it on with the volume all the way down, the way he liked it, and he sat before the television for two hours, staring at the images that appeared on the screen. At around one o'clock, I went to him and told him it was time for the midday prayer. I helped him get to the bathroom and perform his ablutions, and then we went back to the living room. My grandfather smoked a cigarette before praying, and another afterward, then sat in his chair. I told him that guests would be arriving in fifteen minutes. I helped him to his feet once more, took him by the hand, and we made our way to the reception room. My father, mother, brother, sister, and my paternal uncle and aunt and two of their children were already there.

The doorbell rang. Abir entered first, followed by our guests. Abir went to my grandfather and kissed his hand. I looked the reporters over: two young men, and two young women, in their mid-thirties at most. They resembled the elegantly well-groomed married couples in movies. A fragrance of women's perfume wafted from the group. One of the women was exceptionally striking. She was dressed in high heels, which showed off her legs. The other woman wore a contemporary style of *hijab*. They greeted everyone and introduced themselves. I was able to identify the guy I'd talked to on the phone as soon as I heard his voice, and when we met face-to-face, I realized he knew who I was as well. With a sardonic smile, I led them to my grandfather—who said not a word, even when they introduced themselves to him and told him of their origins and who their families were.

I was eager just to get on with the interview, but my father invited our guests to sit and have some tea. Everyone joined in the general conversation about work and life and rising costs in Jordan, and so on.

I glanced at my grandfather; I could tell he wasn't following what was going on around him. Then I saw that one of the reporters was staring at my sister. I glared at him to let him know I could see what he was up to, and he got the message, turning away from her to look in another direction. I was just about to get up, go over to the guy, and belt him one, when my father addressed the guests, indicating my grandfather in his chair. "Please," my father said cordially.

The reporters arranged themselves in a semicircle around my grandfather; I sat beside him. They got out their cameras, papers, and recording equipment, then cleared their throats, ready to get to work. Silence fell, then was broken by the guy who'd called me on the phone. Privately, I wished the guy who'd been ogling my sister was the one taking the lead and putting himself in the line of fire, but it seemed they'd worked it out beforehand who was going to do what.

Rather than come straight to the point, the interviewer went on in a general way about the purpose of the interview before getting into the questions. When I heard the first one, I let out a snicker that annoyed my father, who gave me a look that said, "Knock it off." I nodded and focused on the proceedings. I tried hard to pick out something—anything—original in the program they had come up with. When they got to the end of what they called "the first set of questions," my grandfather was silent. I told the interviewer they would have to leave if my grandfather chose not to talk, but he was determined to get what he'd come for.

The members of the team conferred in whispers for a few moments. Then the interviewer moved to another set of questions. By the time he'd finished, I was wishing I could stand up and ask a few questions of my own—a third set, then a fourth, a fifth, a tenth. I was seething with contempt for these interlopers, and I wished my grandfather could know what was going through my head. I heard the guy saying something about a final question as he reached for a slip of paper that was tucked inside his jacket. If it had been up to me, I'd have snatched the paper from him and pissed on it, but I behaved myself, mindful of the warnings my father had given me beforehand. The interviewer prefaced his final question with a speech about the importance of what my grandfather had to say, rabbiting on about a "war on memory" and the moral significance of the journalists' project. The nerve of the guy, this phony intellectual—he pissed me off. I held up five fingers, to let him know how much time they had left to wrap up the interview. Just then I looked at my grandfather and realized that he was about to say something. The other male reporter stood up, prepared to take pictures, or record a video, while the hot female journalist sat up, poised to write down my grandfather's words. While the interviewer, oblivious, droned on and on with his lead-in to the final question, all of a sudden my grandfather stopped them all cold, shouting, *"Get the hell out of here, you motherfuckers!"*

Qaa'id

IT WAS WHEN I WAS A STUDENT AT YARMOUK UNIVERSITY in Irbid that I discovered by chance that I didn't exactly know the colors of the Palestinian flag. I had foreign friends who were studying Arabic, and I was flirting with an American student, who, whenever she came to the university, always had two *kufiyyahs* in her bag: the red-and-white Jordanian one and the black-and-white Palestinian one. I teased her once about the extreme care she was taking to avoid offense against the territorial allegiances of anyone at the university. I tried to convince her that the students there were less concerned with who wore what sort of *kufiyyah* than they were with the crisis in public transportation that confronted them every morning. The girl rejected my arguments; she thought they were naïve. I told her the reason for her excessive caution was that she knew Jordan and Palestine exclusively from books, whereas I knew the on-the-ground reality of them. "Because you're Palestinian-Jordanian?" she said. I detected a note of sarcasm in her question, but I nodded. She said one had to take precautions.

"What precautions?!"

"I wear the Palestinian *kufiyyah* in my morning class, because the professor is Palestinian. I wear the Jordanian one in my afternoon class because the professor is Jordanian."

"What do you wear in your bedroom?"

"Don't be obnoxious. Right now we're talking about the question of national identity."

"*What* question, you nut?"

"There was a civil war in this country thirty years ago."

"Really? Thanks for filling me in."

"You're not taking anything I say seriously."

"People here have forgotten the whole business, but apparently you're majoring in it."

"People don't forget. They've just repressed it."

Her patronizing tone as she undertook to teach me a lesson on my people and my country wasn't lost on me. *"Shut up,"* I told myself, but she'd got me worked up now. I reached for her bag, opened it up, and pulled out the two *kufiyyahs*. She snatched her bag back and demanded that I return the *kufiyyahs*. I refused. Instead, I draped one over my right shoulder, the other over my left, and told her to follow me. We went to the main entrance of the university, where I walked into the midst of a group of students, my arms half-raised. The girl walked beside me. I kept glancing right and left at the students, who looked back at me, grinning. I turned to the American girl as if to say, "*See?*" She whispered in my ear that we needed to get out of there. I refused. I kept walking.

After a bit, I went and got us two coffees, and we sat down on the sidewalk of a street well out of the way of curious gazes. I demanded that she admit she'd been naïve to be so scrupulous about her *kufiyyahs*. We had walked through a bunch of students, and all they'd done was smile when they saw me. "What more do you want?" I asked her. She shook her head and asked me what made me so sure I was the one the students had been looking at. That pissed me off. I stood up abruptly, but she grabbed my hand and asked that we set aside talk of politics for a while. It was the first time she'd ever spontaneously taken my hand. I interlaced my fingers with hers and said that would depend on how long her hand stayed in mine. Sensing that she'd conceded too much to me, she pulled away. I told her that I had two *kufiyyahs* hanging on the wall of my room, one Palestinian and the other Jordanian, and I invited her to come and have a look at them. She told me my seduction technique was naïve and outdated, something out of the 1970s. Embarrassed, I tried a different tactic. I told her I would lay odds she wore a black bra. She said I was such an idiot that she was actually tempted to go with me. I flagged down a taxi, and we went to my room.

There was, of course, not even one *kufiyyah* on the wall of my room. She started asking me questions about my family history, while I speculated about the best way to get her clothes off. She asked me about the *Nakba,* and when my family had left Palestine; meanwhile, in my head, I was having a different conversation with her.

"Did your family leave in '48 or '67?"

Have you gone out with any Palestinians before me?

"Really? When did your father come to Jordan?"

When did you lose your virginity?

"Do you think the Palestinians in Jordan want to go back to Palestine?"

You think I can concentrate on anything right now besides your breasts?
"Are you in favor of a one-state or a two-state solution?"
Are you in favor of monogamy or polyamory?
"If only the refugee problem could be solved."
If only I could get you to shut up for a while.
I asked her if she wanted anything to drink. She answered in an endearingly sweet and girlish voice. I moved closer to her and pulled her toward me. She didn't stop me. I brought her face close to mine, and was just about to kiss her, when she put her finger on my lips and asked me if I had a Palestinian flag somewhere in my room. *"The hell with Palestine,"* I was thinking, but all I said was, "No." Then shit got real. She asked me the order of the three stripes on the Palestinian flag, top to bottom. I mumbled something and tried again to kiss her.

"Answer me first."

"Black, green, white."

She looked at me in surprise.

"What's your problem?" I said.

Her expression changed. "Fuck you," she said in English.

"White, black, green," I said.

"Fuck you."

"Red, black, white."

"Fuck you."

She picked up her bag and made to leave. There were no smartphones then, no Google I could hastily consult to get myself out of this. I asked her to wait.

"Fuck you."

I ransacked my memory, trying to envision the flag. All at once it struck me that I had never marched in a demonstration or carried a Palestinian flag. And this nutty girl knew the flag better than I did. She yanked open the door at the same moment I said, "White, green, black."

"Fuck you."

"Red, white, black."

"Fuck you."

Purple pink shit lilac brown shit game-over shit the day's lost shit the American girl won't come back shit all because I'm clueless about a piece of cloth . . . *shit.*

Hahahahahahaha

HAHAHAHAHAHAHA! *MOTHERFUCKERS!* HAHAHAHAHAHAHA! My grandfather had exceeded all my expectations. My dear grandfather! Oh, my dear Grandpa . . . me, I'd have just kicked them out, but you, you did better than that—you got your revenge. *Motherfuckers.* All my life my grandfather's been warning me about losers like them. He said I'd meet a lot of people who, on finding out that I was Palestinian, would ask me about my history and the history of my family. These "thieves," as he called them, were always intent on stealing our stories, on writing them down and then putting them on display for the world's entertainment. My grandfather brought me up not to tell. He said he wouldn't tell me anything about his past, so that I couldn't, in a moment of weakness, divulge it to strangers. At first, I didn't begin to understand the reason for his desire to keep his memories to himself, sharing them with no one, but I grew up with this behavior, and it seems I got used to it; I no longer see it as problematic in any way. My father, on the other hand—I've often heard him arguing with my grandfather. Maybe this is why my grandfather loves me so much and keeps me close to him. "You're not like your father," he tells me, adding, "Take care, my boy—mind you don't ever try to find out what happened, my boy."

One time our high school history teacher asked who among us had grandparents still living who were survivors of the *Nakba*. A few hands went up—mine and some of my classmates'. So the teacher asked each of us to go home and write a short essay on memories of the *Nakba* as recounted by a grandfather or grandmother. My grandmother had died before her time, in 1993, at which point my father, as the eldest son, had taken in my grandfather. When I got home from school that day, I approached him and told him what the teacher had asked for. My grandfather said, "Write." I opened a notebook and sat down by him.

"Palestine was lost."

"Palestine was lost."

"Full stop."

"All right."

"Palestine was lost."

"I already wrote that, Grandpa."

"Write it again."

"Okay."

"Period."

"Period."

"Palestine was lost. Period. Palestine was lost. Period. How many pages do you need?"

"At least three."

"Keep going, then. Palestine was lost. Period. Palestine was lost. Period. Palestine was lost. Period."

I turned my three pages in to the teacher. At the next history class, he came in and called on me. He accused me of making fun of him, but I swore that I had questioned my grandfather as instructed, and that this was what my grandfather had said to me. The teacher asked me for details, and I said that my grandfather hadn't given me any. He asked how old my grandfather was, and I told him. He asked me to invite him to the school, but my grandfather rejected this overture. He was still in comparatively good health in those days, but he didn't want to meet the teacher. My beloved grandfather. He hadn't had any formal education, but he could read and write, and it's thanks to him that, from childhood, I developed a love-hate relationship with reading. At the University of Jordan, where I majored in engineering, it turned out my general education was better than that of my classmates. Later I asked my grandfather why he had done what he did with the history teacher, and he said that, as far as he was concerned, the *Nakba* was the loss of Palestine, and beyond that nothing mattered.

The effect of my grandfather's curses on the reporters was huge. For my part, I couldn't contain myself: I laughed out loud, although I tried to hide my face with my hand. The reporters were aware that I shared my grandfather's strange hostility, so they looked to my father for some explanation of what had happened. My father's embarrassment was obvious, but it's not as if I hadn't warned him about how this meeting would turn out. My father knew in his heart that my grandfather didn't have all that much time left to live, and he was still hoping his father would officially let someone in on his secrets, his recollections. My father and his brothers disapproved of my grandfather's way of dealing with his past, and I often heard them complain about his bizarre resistance to the idea of written accounts. My father and uncles were born years after the *Nakba;* accordingly, they regarded my grandfather as a living historical record of great importance, a record that refused to let itself be set down for posterity. The situation was precisely this: my father wanted my grandfather to be transformed into a book, into a document he could show off, maybe, to his friends and acquaintances. When the whole business of a newspaper report came up, my father thought he saw his chance. To him, the journalists represented a great opportunity to persuade my grandfather to change his mind, especially if he could perceive them as Palestine's new generation, motivated by patriotism in pursuing his story. When my grandfather held his peace after the first set of questions had been pitched, my father looked at me, cocked his head toward my grandfather, and pointed his index finger at his lips. I answered him with a gesture to the effect that this was all a waste of time.

The two young women stood up first, then the guy with the camera followed them. The one who'd been asking the questions, though, sat there stunned for a moment, before getting to his feet as well. My father, in an effort to bring this embarrassing episode promptly to a halt, proposed to our guests that they go into the next room for a bit. Everyone filed out, including all the family members except me and my grandfather. I took his hand and kissed it several times, then hugged him. I looked into his eyes and saw a glimmer of tears there. I heard him murmuring, "So the motherfuckers want to know what happened," he said. "As if I'd tell them my stories in a million years. Crap." His voice shook with anger, and I wished it were a little louder, so that the journalists would hear it in the next room. I calmed him down, soothed him, and promised him that this incident wouldn't recur. If only my father had listened to my arguments and not put my beloved grandfather through such an ordeal. Although I could tell it was essential that I stay with him until he calmed down, at the same time I was enormously curious to know what was going on in the next room. *Motherfuckers.* Hahahahahahaha!

Khaa'in

I KEPT WONDERING, AS THE YEARS PASSED, WHICH WAS BETTER: to marry a Palestinian woman and cheat on her with a woman who wasn't Palestinian, or the other way around. I knew the pros and cons of marriage to a Palestinian, but I couldn't make up my mind about it. So I concluded that I would leave it to fate to decide for me. I met the Iraqi woman who would become my wife when she was about to cross the street at Rabieh Circle. I was headed in the other direction when I saw something fall from her hand. I ran over, picked it up, and called out to her. When she turned back, I went over and handed the object to her; ten years later, she still has it. She calls it "our love token." After we got married, my friends began to speculate about the "woman of breeding and propriety" with whom I would betray my wife; that I would be unfaithful was a foregone conclusion. At the University of Jordan, they called me "God's ordained traitor." In Military Science class the lecturer might be explaining the difference between the Warsaw Pact and the NATO Alliance, while I would be using one girlfriend's phone to send a message to my other girlfriend, asking her who was the girl she'd been walking with that morning, on the pretext that I wanted to introduce her to my cousin. I don't believe I stayed in any relationship longer than two weeks. But my relationships during my college years, numerous as they were, didn't go beyond kissing, hugging, nuzzling, and that sort of thing, so I remained a virgin until marriage. I'm not sure, now, whether that was a conscious decision, or whether it was conservative propriety or lack of confidence or what. Although it wasn't for lack of opportunity, I was the opposite of most of my friends in that I didn't go very far in my physical relationships with women. I'm not a physically demonstrative person, if that's the right expression, and to this day I don't enjoy sex itself so much as the process of getting there. Two weeks after I got married, I realized that if I stayed faithful to my wife, I would die without ever having slept with a Palestinian woman. I shared this thought with a male Palestinian friend whom I'd met at the newspaper where I'd started working before my marriage. My friend asked me if it was really necessary to have sex with a Palestinian, especially considering that we were Palestinian; people, he pointed out, weren't always attracted to men or women of their own tribe. I asked him if he had ever slept with a Palestinian. He said he had. I asked him whether there was anything different about the experience.

"Different from what?"

"I don't know. Just different."

"I don't get this obsession of yours with the idea of having sex with a Palestinian."

"It's not so much the sex I'm interested in—I just want to try out all that poetry we were brought up on . . ."

"That stuff you've been reading will be the ruin of you."

"The woman, the motherland, etcetera, etcetera. You follow me?"

"What I 'follow' is that you've been married just two weeks, and you should be ashamed of yourself for thinking like this."

An odd thing happened to me a month after that conversation. I met a Palestinian girl, an employee at the Madina Street branch of Arab Bank. The moment I gave her my ID, as I was about to make a deposit to my account, I was sure I was going to sleep with her. The night before, my wife had caught me off guard with a lovemaking session that made me all the more certain I would have to cheat on her as soon as possible. The clock read ten minutes to three when I entered the bank, and the lobby was nearly empty. I noted that the young woman wasn't wearing a ring. When I caught the scent of her perfume, I knew instantly what kind it was. I brought my face right up to the teller window, and said, "That's expensive perfume you're wearing." If her monthly salary, I added, sufficed for her to buy such perfume, then it must surely also allow her to treat a hardworking newspaperman to a cup of coffee. She was taken aback by my brashness, but I could see by the look in her eye that what made the biggest impression on her was that I had recognized her perfume. The following evening we were at a café, and I was telling her how beautiful my wife was. We went on talking and meeting for a month, and then she asked me to leave her alone; she wasn't interested in getting too involved in a relationship that could go nowhere. I agreed, on one condition.

"Sleep with me first."

"You're insane. Do you have no shame at all?"

"Who cares? Afterward you'll be rid of me, I promise."

To this day I have no idea where I got the guts to make a demand like that. In her place, I would have spat in the face of such an impudent bastard and walked out. To my astonishment, however, she took me by the hand and conducted me to the Grand Hyatt Hotel in Jabal Amman. She paid for one night, and we went upstairs.

When we got to the room, I told her that the whole point of this for me was the need to make it with a Palestinian. She laughed uneasily and told me what an idiot I was. I spoke in a no-nonsense manner, as though I was conducting a chemistry experiment. I told her I would feel as if my life had been missing something if it ended without my ever having had sex with a Palestinian. It wasn't a question for me of some conviction that Palestinian women were different from other women, merely a desire to have, in the course of my life, every possible experience with Palestinians. My mother, my father, and all of my siblings were Palestinian, I had Palestinian friends, I read Palestinian authors, I'd eaten and drunk with Palestinians, fought with Palestinians, cursed out Palestinians, traveled with Palestinians, stolen from Palestinians, and on and on. Did it make any sense that I should die without ever seeing a Palestinian woman naked in my bed?

"So why didn't you marry a Palestinian, then?"

I had no ready answer to that question, but I found myself telling her that I hadn't wanted to replicate my parents' experience. I didn't want my household to turn into another Palestinian saga. We slept and woke to news of Palestine; we ate it, drank it, debated it, swore at it. She said this was a very strange attitude, suggesting that I had become disengaged from Palestine. I told her I was, on the contrary, abnormally engaged, as my presence there with her at that moment testified. She asked me whether I would like to see Palestine. Sliding my hand under her skirt, I said there was more than one way of seeing Palestine. She laughed and asked me whether I was going to cheat on my wife with other Palestinian women after her. I told her it was up to her now to convince me that there was no need.

When we left the hotel, she entreated me not to keep pursuing her, and I gave her my promise. As she told me goodbye, she said I was the shallowest Palestinian she'd ever met in her life.

The Eldest Son

GOD FORGIVE YOU, MY FATHER. I was expecting you to react by refusing to talk, but I never foresaw anything so extreme. I was acutely embarrassed in the presence of our guests, who had committed no offense deserving of such treatment as this. All right, some of them seemed arrogant, but in the end they were just doing their jobs. When will my father open up his locked vault? For so long now I've been begging him to let me document his youth in Palestine. I've told him repeatedly that it would gratify my children to learn the truth of what happened from their own grandfather's lips.

"Gratify them? Palestine was lost."

That continued to be his default response. Palestine was lost. Every time we asked him a question about the past, his reply was, "Palestine was lost." I know. I swear to God, I know. We all know. But we know few of the details as to how it was lost. We don't know the details of your own personal loss, Papa. We don't know the stories of our village at the time when everyone left it: who the casualties were, who among those who were driven out made it to safety, and who didn't. This is our right, Papa. You were nearly grown at the time, and there must be a great deal you could tell us. Age fifteen—that's old enough for a person to have a veritable archive of amassed stories not dimmed by the passage of time. My mother herself didn't know the story of her husband's background. My father got to know her family, who were living in the camp at Jenin, in the 1950s. He married the daughter, and moved with her to the Balata camp, near Nablus. They were there until the *Naksa* in 1967, when they emigrated to Amman. The *Naksa*, now—about *that* I've heard plenty. My mother told me all about it, and her doing so upset my father, but he didn't want to impose his views on her. Only my father's *Nakba* has remained obscure, concealed from my siblings and me. When my father heard my mother telling us stories about the *Naksa*, the occupation, Nasser, and his defeat, he laughed bitterly.

"*This* is 'occupation,'" he said. "*Naksa*, occupation. Occupations come and go. Occupation isn't the *Nakba*. There was a *Nakba*, in '48. The

Nakba isn't occupation. Nablus was still Nablus. '67 wasn't a *Nakba*. You can't know what *'Nakba'* means unless you know what happened in '48." Exactly—exactly! I stopped him the instant he spoke these words. It was one of the few times I ever raised my voice to my father. I shouted at him, "I do want to know! Papa, I want to know! For pity's sake, please tell me—I'm begging you!" He made to stand up and go to his room, but I seized him by his shoulders. "You're not going anywhere, Papa." He glared at me, gave me a shove, and went.

My father opened a small grocery store in Jabal Amman, an enterprise he maintained from 1968 until a few years after my mother died. After her death, I insisted that he move in with me. He closed the shop when he got too tired to keep it going, taking nothing with him but a map of Palestine, which had hung on the wall there and now assumed a new place on the wall of his room in my house. After the Oslo Accords and the Israel-Jordan Peace Treaty, some Palestinians began obtaining visas to visit Palestine from the Israeli Embassy in Amman. I held no clear political position on the matter; I had always been pragmatic, not delving too much into politics—plus I think my father's stance on his past had dampened my curiosity. I did love reading, and I'd read some of the works of Ghassan Kanafani and Mahmoud Darwish, as well as memoirs by the leaders of Fatah and other such material, but I had never settled on a clearly defined set of opinions. I wasn't for PFLP or Fatah or Hamas. I believed in Palestine, same as other Palestinians in the diaspora, but, in that connection, my personal and professional life never involved any activism. Now it occurred to me to suggest to my father that he apply for a visa to visit Palestine, and I thought about going with him if he agreed.

"Visa from where?"

"From the Israeli Embassy in Amman."

"There's only one reason I'd ever go to the Embassy."

"And what's that?"

"To take a shit on its doorstep."

Great. Thanks, Papa. Keep all those feelings pent up inside you, and don't talk to us about Palestine. All through the second intifada we sat in front of the television, which was showing footage of the "'48 Palestinians"—those living inside the 1948 mandate—who fell while demonstrating in solidarity with those in occupied West Bank and Gaza.

I looked at my father and felt that he was following the details with more than his usual interest. I wanted to provoke him, so I grabbed the remote and turned off the television. He rounded angrily on me and told me to turn it back on. I refused, saying that if there was no need for us to know the details then he could do without them as well. Palestine was lost, and that was that. It embarrasses me now to admit that saying these things to him filled me with a vindictive satisfaction. I wanted him to have the same experience he'd forced on me by keeping silent about his past. Going red in the face, his voice rising, he demanded again that I turn on the television.

"Why? This is news about the '48 Palestinians. 1948 . . . remember that year? Does it mean something to you? Personally, I don't know much about it. What about you? Are you actually from Palestine? Can you prove it?"

"I made a mistake, agreeing to live with you. To hell with you, and to hell with 1948."

"Fine. Palestine was lost. Don't forget that. Palestine was lost, and so were you, and so were we. What else do you want?"

"I want to leave your house."

"Oh, no, you're not going anywhere. You're not leaving, Papa. You left Palestine—wasn't that enough? One experience of exile you refuse to tell anyone about is sufficient. Keep it hidden, Papa, keep it hidden."

He came over to me and slapped my face. I don't recall that he'd ever, since my childhood, struck me, and now here I was—a tall, broad-shouldered young man, married, a professional engineer—and here was my father, hitting me, and Palestine was lost, and your stories, Papa, stayed buried.

When Abir told us about the newspaper profile that some of her friends wanted to put together, the desire to learn about my father reawakened in me. He had reached the age of eighty-five, and I hardly knew him. I had no interest in getting his opinion on the idea of the proposed report, as I was certain he would refuse. I placed certain conditions on the meeting, to which the reporters agreed. I didn't sleep the night before the interview. Naturally, I was hoping my father would talk, but at the same time I could imagine the pain it would cause me if it was to others—to these strangers—rather than his own family, that he told the stories I had been hoping for decades to hear. I imagined various ways the meeting might play out, but my imagination was not equal to the reality that was my father. I told myself that I was putting him face-to-face with a different generation of Palestinians who wanted to hear what he had to say, and that maybe this would rouse something in him. Perhaps, sensing how little time was left to him before he departed this world forever, he would decide to reveal the stories of that other, earlier departure. Perhaps he would realize that his words, passing beyond the narrow confines of our family and appearing in a respected newspaper, would reach thousands of readers, who, thanks to his narrative, would become acquainted with a Palestinian history obscure to so many. Perhaps. Perhaps.

Khaa'ina

THE MUSICIANS WE'D HIRED FOR OUR WEDDING were just about to begin performing when I saw a member of the band whispering in the bandleader's ear. I was standing beside my new husband, family members clustered around us in the lobby of the hotel. I think it was around 7:40 in the evening, and we'd intended, after the processional, to go to the room designated for taking pictures. When the leader of the band began conferring with the other players, my brother came over and asked my husband why the processional was starting late. He said he had no idea. Some of the family had begun hesitantly to sing, as if to encourage the Palestinian performers to get on with the show, when all of a sudden the bandleader raised his hand and at his signal the room fell quiet. He picked up a microphone and said, "We are obliged, regretfully, to cancel our performance."

My husband and I are distantly related. I met him at a dinner at my cousin's place and found out later that the whole idea had been to fix us up. We went out a few times, and we got along well. I was looking for a job, having graduated from college, when the relationship came along and rescued me from the dullness of my daily life. Before long we were engaged, and my father insisted that we set an early wedding date. We checked out some hotels in a moderate price range, and settled on the Amman International, on Jordan University Street. We were determined that the marriage should take place before prices skyrocketed in the high-season months of June and July. The manager of the hotel discussed various options with us, the most expensive of which was to offer the guests a buffet supper. I waited for my fiancé to put in a word, since he would be footing the bill. I could see droplets of sweat beginning their descent from his forehead.

"Does the price include the band for the processional as well?"

"No. That will vary according to what sort of performers are hired."

"We want Palestinians."

"That's fine, but the band we work with is expensive. The Egyptian one is cheaper."

My fiancé took me aside and suggested we make do with the Egyptian band. I told him my family would absolutely refuse, because the wedding was, for them, an occasion of national significance. He thought that I was showcasing my family's loyalty to Palestine, and insisted that his family, too, would prefer the Palestinian band, but that he wanted the decision to be ours. I told him we would only get married once, and that we needed to do all we could to satisfy our families' wishes as well as our own. We went back and resumed our conversation with the manager. We asked him whether it would be possible to lower the cost of the Palestinian band if we reduced the time given over to the processional. The manager looked at us with ill-concealed distaste, and said it wasn't necessary to go to all this fuss.

"It is—believe me, it is."

"What do you want, exactly?"

"Let's keep the processional to just fifteen minutes, rather than half an hour."

"Are there particular songs you'd like to cut?"

My fiancé said he would leave that up to the performers, but I interrupted, saying that they at least had to include the song "Where to? To Ramallah," since my family came from Ramallah. The manager made a note of this and asked my fiancé where his family was from. He said they were from Acre.

"Unfortunately, there are no songs about Acre."

"On the contrary," I said, "there's the song 'From Acre Prison Came a Funeral.'"

Having delivered this flippant remark, I laughed, to let my fiancé know I was only joking. The manager snickered.

We returned to the subject of food. The manager said there were three options: cake and juice, "snack," or the buffet. We asked him about the "snack." He explained that it was a selection that would be laid out on a table, a spread consisting of salads and hors d'oeuvres, such as spinach and meat pies. And the buffet? The price of this would vary depending on whether we wanted to include lamb. Was *kunaafa* available? It was. I wanted a sumptuous dinner, but I left the decision to the esteemed engineer: my penny-pinching fiancé. He turned to me and whispered in my ear that perhaps, after all, the main purpose of the wedding was the night that, for us, would follow it, and that our guests' stomachs should be the least of our worries. I suggested he include a disclaimer on the wedding invitations stipulating that they were valid only on condition that the guests eat their dinners before attending. That made him so angry he nearly left. I realized that I had better whip up a bit of romance in the wake of all this tension. I whispered in his ear that it would be enough for me if we shared just a glass of water—but for the conventions that had to be satisfied, I said, I wouldn't have asked for a wedding in the first place. He calmed down a little. I took him by the hand and caressed his fingers. Men, I thought to myself, were bigger idiots than we women could imagine, their control over the world since its creation the greatest mystery of all time.

"Cake and juice will be fine," we told the manager. The expression I read in his face said, "Kiss my ass."

The bandleader's bizarre announcement put everyone on edge. My brother advanced on the man with a look that demanded an explanation from him. Forestalling my brother's approach, the leader spoke again into the microphone, saying that it turned out today was the sixtieth anniversary of the *Nakba,* and it would be disrespectful for his band to sing on such a day. Silence descended on the room. We didn't know what to say. My husband dropped my hand and went over and spoke to the bandleader for a few minutes, and then rejoined me. The manager of the hotel got involved, trying to salvage the situation by offering a substantial refund if we would concede the processional and go directly to the room set aside for photographs. He begged us not to tell anyone what had happened. At this point I worked up my nerve and started to make my way over toward the bandleader to ask him to perform songs about the *Nakba*. My husband, however, grabbed my hand and, cursing, maneuvered me into an elevator, which would convey us to where the photographer awaited us.

The guests tried to carry on as if the wedding was proceeding normally. My father pretended to pay no attention to what had happened, although his eyes gave away his anger with himself and with us. When the wedding was over, I went to my mother and embraced her, thanking her for this *Nakba* of a wedding. Everyone put the blame on everyone else for not having taken note of the coincidence of our wedding with the fateful anniversary of the *Nakba*. I was impatient for my husband and myself to get to our room, so that I could let out what I was holding inside. After we'd said goodbye to everyone, I threw myself on the bed, saying nothing but, "Good night." My poor husband approached me and tried to soothe me, but I ignored him. When he began unbuttoning my wedding dress, I shouted at him to get away from me, adding that all the armies in the world couldn't make me sleep with him on the anniversary of the *Nakba*. It was 11:30 by then, so he told me he could wait a half hour for the start of a new day, when the anniversary of the *Nakba* would be behind us. He struck me then as nothing but a fool, and I found that my desire for him had diminished alarmingly. I told him he had better leave me the hell alone if he didn't want his wedding night to turn into an actual *Nakba*.

In the morning, I woke up calmer. Feeling sorry for my new husband, I woke him up as well. "Good *Nakba* morning to you, sweetie," I said. After that, every year, on the anniversary of the *Nakba*, I would make it a point to cheat on my husband.

And Then What?

I WAS STILL PRACTICALLY A BABY when my grandfather came to live with us. And while politics wasn't a very significant part of our lives, he insisted all the same on maintaining his mocking, adversarial stance toward anyone who wanted to know "what happened." Whenever there was some kind of disaster, or a war broke out somewhere in the world, my grandfather would shake his head as he listened to the news, and remark that soon the "story thieves" would be after those poor souls, too. I was in my senior year of high school in 2003, at the time of the second Gulf War and the American occupation of Iraq. Amman filled up with Iraqis, and I befriended some of them. Once, one of them visited me at home, and I introduced him to the family. When my grandfather greeted him, he began with the usual pleasantries, but then went on, "Don't be like us. Don't give them any stories." My friend shook his head, amazed; I signaled him to leave the subject alone. My grandfather's comments were repeated during the 2006 war in Lebanon, but they reached a fever pitch with the Arab Spring. He wasn't much interested in knowing the effects of one demonstration or another, and at times his cold disinterest mystified me. The one thing that preoccupied him was that those "poor souls" were destined to become mere repositories packed with memories on which others might pounce. In the end I got used to my grandfather and his wary, defensive stance, which I adopted without contesting it, particularly since it meant he would talk to me, and explain things to me.

My father wasn't very happy when he saw that I could stand up to him, asking him to stop harassing my grandfather when they argued about anything to do with the past. He accused me of imbecility for parroting my grandfather's statements. He said that if the Palestinians all followed my grandfather's advice, no one would know their story, and Palestine would vanish from the map of the world. One time my grandfather overheard one of these exchanges. He waited until I went to my room, then called me.

"What does your father want?"

"He wants me not to listen to you."

"Why?"

"He says the Palestinians lost everything, and that nothing was left to them but their memories. He says our duty is to preserve our memories for coming generations, so that the world will know what happened."

"And then what?"

"What?"

"So the world finds out what happened. What then?"

I didn't have an answer for him. He took my hand and began to talk—and talk and talk and talk.

"Here's a story. There were a hundred people in the village and the Jews came. They lined us up against the wall and began kicking the shit out of us. Then someone named Abu Muhammad called out to them that our Arab allies were coming, they were on their way. One of the soldiers said to him, 'You can shove it up your ass, you and your "Arab allies,"' and punched him. Then they told us we had forty-eight hours to clear out of the village. You follow me? And then the village was lost."

My grandfather paused, as though to assess the impact of his words on me. I was stunned. I couldn't believe my grandfather was talking. I stared at him, astonished. I was nearly on the point of going and calling my father, when my grandfather resumed speaking.

"Or here's a story. There were a hundred and thirty-three people in the village, and we heard the news about Deir Yassine. The *mukhtar* called the men of the village to an assembly in his meetinghouse, to discuss what should be done. I was fifteen years old, and they didn't let me join the meeting, but I stood outside at the window and heard everything. The men were divided into factions. One group said we had to stay and take up arms, while the other said we'd better get out before those bastards came to massacre us and rape our women. In the end, it was the second group who carried the day. And then the village was lost."

For a moment I was completely confused. I opened my mouth to point out to him that the first story wasn't the same as the second one, that they contradicted each other, and that I didn't know which one was the truth. But now there was no stopping him.

"Or here's a story. The Jews came to our village before they went to Deir Yassine, and surrounded all of our houses one by one. They fired their guns and ranted and raved through their megaphones, telling us they were going to fuck us one after the other. With my very own eyes I saw the village elders lying on the ground in their own blood. My father told me to go, to take my mother and my brothers and sisters and run for it. I carried my mother, and we left the village by the east side. And then the village was lost.

"Or here's a story. We gathered in the village square when we heard that the Jews were getting close. We broke up into groups. Those of us who were under eighteen were posted to guard the well and the mosque. While I was at the well, I heard gunfire. To tell you the truth, I was so scared I pissed myself. The army started speaking through megaphones, telling us to surrender. The villagers all refused to surrender and kept resisting until they were martyred. Then the village was lost.

"Or here's a story. The Jews actually came and asked us, 'What do you say you stay in Palestine, and don't take up arms against us?' We looked at each other, and of course we refused, determined to resist. When the Arab Liberation Army came, they asked for volunteers. My friends and I went to volunteer, but they sent us back because we were too young. Everyone who was over eighteen joined the Liberation Army. The only ones left behind were women, children, boys under eighteen, and a few animals. When the Jews came in force we had no way of stopping them. We ran with all the rest who'd run. Then the village was lost.

"Here's a story. Here's a story. Here's a story. Here's a story." I didn't interrupt him, even though now I wished he would stop.

That was the first and last time my grandfather talked to me about the *Nakba*. After the third iteration, I saw the point he was making, and started keeping track of the number of stories. When an hour and a half had gone by and the tally was up to forty-eight, he said, "Now go tell your esteemed father these stories—maybe that will get him off my back. But after he's enjoyed listening to all the stories, tell him one more thing: Palestine was lost."

Mutarjima

HOW MY TEARS FLOWED AS I HEAVED THE PAN of *maqlouba* into the trash! I had followed my grandmother's instructions exactly: Cut up the chicken and put it at the bottom of the pot. Place the eggplant on top, and then the rice. But then I decided I wanted to be a little more creative, so I added a layer of cauliflower, and then the rice on top of that. I swear I didn't turn the heat up too high—I swear! It had been cooking for half an hour when the guests arrived.

This was the first year I'd spent outside of Jordan, after I graduated from the university. I'd gotten a job as a translator at a media company in Dubai, and I considered myself lucky to have landed there in the pleasant month of January. The lovely weather made it easy for me to familiarize myself with the city quickly, plus I had friends of various nationalities already working for the same company, and that helped, too. I lived alone in the neighborhood of Mirdif, well away from the hustle and bustle of the city, and I bought a cheap car, mindful of my limited means. In the evenings I went out. Most of my friends were Arabs, but there were also a few Europeans and one American. I was the only Palestinian of the lot, and once, when the subject of food came up, an Egyptian guy who was with us mentioned that the Palestinians took excessive pride in their *maqlouba,* even though it was "nothing but a bit of rice." I replied that it wasn't that we were overly proud, but that it was a truly delicious dish, calling for a skilled cook, because its preparation was such a subtle procedure. I went on in this vein, trying to establish that it wasn't just "a bit of rice," as the Egyptian had claimed, but then the American asked me what, exactly, this *maqlouba* was, and how it was made. As I was explaining it to him, it occurred to me that I had never made *maqlouba* on my own before. I had watched my mother make it many times, but my own role was merely that of an assistant, one with rather limited responsibilities. I tried to be cautious in my response to the American, so as not to get myself into trouble. But the Egyptian, that provocateur, was shrewd enough to discern my discomfiture. He asked me if the rice could be put in first, at the bottom of the pot. I said no, but he said he had Palestinian friends who did this, that he had tasted their *maqlouba*, and that it was quite delicious. Wanting to shift from defense to offense, I replied sarcastically that in that case "delicious" *maqlouba* could hardly be just "a bit of rice," as he had alleged. Two of my female colleagues, one Syrian and one Iraqi, came to my defense, and all at once it became a battle of the sexes. The Egyptian insisted that my hesitation in describing the preparation of *maqlouba* proved that I'd never made it in my life, and therefore I could say nothing on the subject with any authority. On the contrary, I told him: I could, right then, go home and make it for them all in an hour. Although I didn't at that moment realize it, I'd fallen into my own trap, for the Egyptian stood up and challenged me, asking whether this was a genuine invitation. He looked around at the faces of his companions. There were ten of us, young women and men. Ten. What sort of mess had I got myself into? The clock said 7:00 p.m.; it was Thursday, so we had the next day off. The group went silent, all eyes expectantly on me to see how I would react. I was cornered—there was no retreat.

It was agreed that they would catch up with me at home at precisely nine o'clock; I promised them that the food would be ready by ten. I made a hasty departure from the coffee shop where we'd met, and headed for one of Dubai's enormous malls to buy what I needed. On the way there, I kept trying to call my mother, but she wasn't picking up—this was before the era of smartphones and social media apps. I called my older sister, who didn't answer the phone either. I was getting increasingly anxious. Was eggplant the only option? Potatoes might be easier. I remembered that I had no rice at all at home, as I'd done scarcely any cooking since coming to Dubai. Did I even have cooking oil? Salt and pepper? There was no time for me to go home and see what supplies I had on hand, so I decided to buy everything. I opened my bag, only to discover that I didn't have enough money with me. When I got to the mall, I found an ATM and withdrew two thousand dirhams. I tried again to call my mother, but it was no use. I called my aunt on my father's side, my aunt on my mother's side, the wife of a paternal uncle, the wife of a maternal uncle, a cousin—nothing. I started to cry. I called my father and was overjoyed when he answered. I asked him to pass the phone to my mother immediately. He said they were at a wedding, and that she wouldn't be able to talk to me because the music was too loud. I asked him if he knew the exact recipe for *maqlouba*.

"That's what this is about?" he asked. "If that's all you wanted, I'm going to hang up now."

"Papa!" Surely he could hear that I was crying! "Please, Papa—it's an emergency! *Maqlouba*, Papa—please. *Maqlouba*. Let me talk to Mama. *Maqlouba*. I'm begging you."

My father said nothing—perhaps he was trying to work out whether these tears of mine could really be on account of *maqlouba*—and a moment later my mother came on the line. I asked her to send me a message with a detailed recipe for *maqlouba*. She told me her phone couldn't send messages outside Jordan. I asked her what time she'd be going home, but then I realized that the wedding celebration had only just begun. My mother told me that my grandmother hadn't come along to the wedding, so I could call and talk to her if I wanted to.

After the conversation with my mother, I hesitated over whether to call my grandmother, with whom I hadn't spoken in more than six months. I decided to buy all the groceries I needed first. Wracking my brain to remember everything, I made my way along all the food aisles. Rice, cooking oil, butter, salt, pepper, spices, eggplant, cauliflower, chicken, tomatoes, cucumber, lemon, yogurt, olive oil. I filled my shopping cart, proceeded to the cashier, and paid. I got home at about eight o'clock and called my grandmother. She refused to give me any information if I didn't explain to her why all of a sudden, at eight o'clock on a Thursday evening, I was asking how to make *maqlouba*. I told her I had invited some friends over, and that they wanted to taste a Palestinian dish. She asked me whether any of them were men. I lied. "No," I said, "no men." She didn't believe me. If all of them had been women, she said, then I wouldn't have felt the need to be so careful about preparing the dish to perfection. I was ready to throw the phone at the wall, turn off all the lights, and go to bed—just go to sleep and forget about this whole fiasco. My grandmother wanted the truth, and all I wanted from her was a few words about *maqlouba*. I swore by how fervently I missed her that the guests were all women. She said if I missed her so much then why hadn't I called her for so long? In my head, I asked of God that *maqlouba* be lost to the Palestinians, just as Palestine was lost to us.

After vigorous apologies on my part and promises to be constantly in touch with her from now on, my grandmother revealed to me the secrets of how to prepare *maqlouba*.

Everyone arrived at around twenty past nine. They sat in the living room, laughing and enjoying themselves, while I struggled to conceal my anxiety about how my *maqlouba* was going to turn out. The wretched Egyptian asked me about the history of *maqlouba,* and I answered him coldly that I didn't know and I didn't want to know. He acted surprised that I, a Palestinian, wouldn't want to learn about the history of her country, in light of Palestine's special circumstances. I restrained myself from asking him about the "special circumstances" that had turned him into such a crashing bore, not to mention a boor, meddling in what did not concern him. Some of the others offered to give me a hand, but I told them everything was under control. That was when an evil smell began seeping into the living room. The Egyptian shook his head and laughed, while the Syrian gestured to me to follow her into the kitchen. There the odor was even stronger. She suggested I check the pot. I asked her whether this smell indicated that the food had burned. She said that was the most likely explanation. She checked the heat setting and asked me how long the pot had been on the burner. When I answered her, she was unable to contain her laughter, despite her obvious sympathy with me. I asked her if there was any way to salvage whatever might be salvaged. We took the lid off the pot, each of us tasted a spoonful of the contents, and then we stood there looking at each other. Now my concern was all about muffling my own sobs, so that the guests—especially that Egyptian prick—wouldn't hear me. The Syrian woman indicated that the only solution was to tell everyone the honest truth about what had happened. I picked up the pot, just as it was; as I set it on the table before my assembled guests, I must have looked like someone condemned to death who'd just entered the courtroom for the last time. I gave them all three minutes to get out of my house. The Egyptian approached me, and I shrieked. The rest of them dragged him by the arm, while he tried to tell me that he only wanted to know what had gone wrong. What I wanted was the lot of them out of my house before I discarded the *maqlouba*. My phone rang moments after they were all gone—it was my grandmother. She asked how the *maqlouba* was.

Motherfuckers?

OUF! "MOTHERFUCKERS!" AN INSULT LIKE A PUNCH IN THE GUT. I was at a loss, with no idea how to respond. Glancing at my colleagues, I saw that all of them had their eyes fastened to the floor. It was a humiliating position we found ourselves in, at once infuriating and abhorrent. I felt as though each of us was waiting for someone else to make the first move to resolve the impasse at which we'd all arrived. I saw Khaa'in mopping sweat from his brow; Khaa'ina had her head in her hands; Mutarjima had turned off her recorder. The eldest son, our host, was silent, as were the others present. But no—there *was* a sound. I looked around to see what it was, and what I saw was the grandson trying to hide his laughter behind his hands. The bastard was snickering—the son of a bitch was *snickering*. Now I was convinced there'd been some sort of conspiracy to subject us to this gross insult; it seemed we'd fallen into a trap set by this family of lunatics. I was overcome by a desire to retaliate, to avenge our professional dignity, which the old man had trampled.

"Could someone explain to us what's going on here?"

The eldest son took me to the next room, and my friends followed. He apologized profusely for what his father had said. He seemed sincere, but I wasn't satisfied. Mutarjima asked whether we had committed some gaffe that was offensive to the family or the old man, and the eldest son said no. Khaa'in spoke up.

"It's bizarre, what's happened," he said. "Did your father know the reason for our visit?"

"Well . . . no, in fact. We didn't tell him."

"Then you're the motherfuckers, not us."

"Listen, I don't want things to get any worse than they already are. I'm going to pretend I didn't hear the remark you just made. Once again, we apologize. I think you'd better go now."

"No, we're not going anywhere." It was Khaa'ina who'd spoken, startling the eldest son with the sharpness of her tone. "We won't leave until we know what it was that made your father so angry. Your own son was standing there next to him, laughing. Something's off here. Did you all plan this whole thing?"

"Of course not. But I couldn't explain even if I wanted to, and I don't. I'm under no obligation to explain anything to you. What do you want? A written apology? Some sort of propitiatory offering? Please, let's just drop it."

"Just one question. Did you know your father was going to behave this way?"

"No, of course I didn't."

"Was it more or less what you were expecting, though? That he would refuse, for example? Something about the newspaper assignment we came here to complete that he would have objected to?"

"Listen to me. I've said all I can. It's not a big deal. All right, so you got cursed out by an old man. What's the problem?"

"There's more to it than just the insult."

"Leave my house, I'm begging you."

"Could we talk to your father again?"

"No!" the son exclaimed furiously. "No, that's it—enough, please! Goodbye."

"Calm down, man. We're just trying to get some answers."

"Haha—that's hilarious. That's all you want? Just some answers? Do you have any idea how many years I've spent wanting the same thing? Ha! Answers, they say—they want answers. Fine. Go for it—someday, God willing."

We looked uncertainly at one another. We still understood nothing. Mutarjima turned and headed for the door, followed by Khaa'ina. Khaa'in looked at me as much to ask whether we shouldn't just go. Then I had an idea. We walked toward the main door, as if about to leave, but then I turned back toward the room where we'd tried to hold the interview and stepped through the door. The eldest son caught up with me and grabbed my arm, trying to restrain me, but I slipped his grasp, hurried over to the old man, and positioned myself in front of him.

The grandson stood up and opened his mouth, but before he could get a word out I said, "Just one question, and then we'll go." On hearing my voice, my colleagues turned around as one, came back, and joined me in the room. "We don't want any trouble," I said. "But why, 'ammi, did you insult us?"

II

1

FOR THREE DAYS THE JOURNALISTS ALL AVOIDED referring to the incident. They didn't meet without other people around, made no eye contact with one another, and kept mum. They threw themselves into their work and their private lives as if nothing was amiss. But in their own minds none of them had the slightest doubt that, before long, they'd be drawn back to the matter at hand, their curiosity irresistibly piqued. The breaking point came even sooner than they'd expected, when their editor-in-chief sent Qaa'id an email message, asking him to set up a meeting with him and the team, so that he could get an update on their progress with the article, and hear how the interview with the old man had gone. Laughing to himself, Qaa'id had to admit they were in for it now. Thinking it best to alert his colleagues informally first of all, he wasted no time picking up his phone. He opened WhatsApp and sent his three team members a message saying, "Urgent meeting." He followed this up with a line or two in which he summarized the message from the boss. The responses from his colleagues arrived in quick succession:

"What are we going to do?"

"We have to get our story straight."

"Should we lie?"

"Not necessarily. We can dress up the truth a little without lying outright."

"Why not say the project never got off the ground in the first place, because the interview was canceled at the last minute?"

"I'm not on board with that. He could find out what happened from some other source."

"Don't forget—we took two days off right before the meeting with the old man, in order to prepare for it. Everyone at the newspaper knows we're supposed to be busy working on an important report for the paper on an eyewitness to the *Nakba*."

"I think we should tell him everything, and let the chips fall where they may."

"Everything?"

"Yes, I know, but if we leave out the part about the old man's outburst, then how do we explain his refusal to talk to us?"

For fifteen minutes they batted the problem back and forth. In the end, they all agreed that Qaa'id had no choice but to send a reply to the boss and arrange a meeting with the team. The meeting time was set for two days later, which gave them more time for deliberation. Khaa'ina suggested via WhatsApp that they gather in the evening at Turtle Green Café to discuss the incident. Mutarjima pointed out that they should come up with a different location, since the last time they'd convened before going to see the old man had been at the Turtle Green Café. Khaa'in proposed Maestro Bar in Jabal al-Luweibdeh, but Mutarjima objected that she didn't frequent bars.

"Should we meet at your house, then? Midnight suits me."

"Could you try not to be such a creep?"

"What's the matter? You can keep your *hijab* on if you want."

"Save the clever repartee," Qaa'id interjected. "Eight o'clock tonight, at Gloria Jean's in Madina Street."

"Okay."

"Okay."

"Okay."

Qaa'id was as startled by how quickly everyone agreed to his suggestion as were his friends that their colleague was now in fact the leader of the team. There was nothing to distinguish him from the others, apart from a certain eloquence, perhaps—indeed it was on this account that they'd elected him as their spokesperson. It was five years earlier that they'd all become friends, around the time each of them had joined the staff at the newspaper, in 2013. Initially, Khaa'in had been attracted to Khaa'ina, but on further acquaintance the two of them had agreed to keep their friendship platonic, so as to maintain the integrity of their professional connection. Qaa'id had made a trio of them the following year, in the course of a birthday party for Khaa'in. The young woman and two young men had joined forces readily enough, united as they were by their Palestinian origin, as well as by their thoroughly liberal outlook and the intensely sardonic wit they directed at everything. Of the three of them, Qaa'id was most at leisure, since he was unencumbered by family obligations at the end of the workday, so when the frequent cancellation of social arrangements started to annoy him, he decided to expand their clique. After looking around for an unattached female to join their ranks—in the interest of gender parity—he told them about a calm, self-possessed young woman at the office, who spoke several languages and apparently knew how to cook.

"How do you know she can cook?"

"She brings her lunch every day, and never orders out."

A few months after Mutarjima became a part of the group, they told her the story of her alleged culinary skills. They were baffled when she reacted by laughing hysterically. Because she wore a *hijab,* Mutarjima imposed on them some constraints as to where they could go, but Qaa'id found her to be a pleasant and cultured companion—and besides, like him, she was single. After Mutarjima joined their cohort, they agreed to meet every Wednesday at Turtle Green Café, whether or not they had a particular reason to get together. Their bond deepened quickly, and they came to know a great deal about one another. They discussed politics, soccer, their work, the economy, love, and religion. The three initial members of the group were surprised to find that Mutarjima adhered to the five daily prayers, but she told them what was surprising was their reaction.

"Unfortunately," said Khaa'in, "you're off my list—I don't sleep with devout women."

Mutarjima threw a glass of water at him, but it missed. As for Khaa'in, for all his apparent levity, the truth was that he was secretly fascinated by the question of whether or not Mutarjima had ever had sex. He kept asking Qaa'id to tell him whether she was still a virgin. "Give me a break, man," said Qaa'id, "we're just friends." Khaa'in replied that sex could improve a friendship, and that devout women in particular were a mystery he hoped to probe. The four friends' family lives were kept separate from their gatherings, and none of them had previously visited any of the others at home.

Qaa'id arrived at Gloria Jean's right on time; Khaa'in showed up last. To make up for his lateness he offered to buy his colleagues whatever they wanted to drink, but he swore at them when they accepted.

They sat on the spacious café's second floor and had been joking around for a bit before they realized that they were avoiding talking about the incident with the old man. Qaa'id cast his eyes sharply around the group. "So?" he said. Mutarjima said she thought they were blowing things out of proportion, that the boss would laugh when he heard what had happened and tell them to forget about it. They didn't spend a lot of time debating the point, simply agreeing to tell the story in its entirety, and declare themselves not responsible for the fact that the project had to be aborted. Khaa'ina said little, and when Qaa'id asked her why she was so quiet, she replied that she was thinking about what had been going on in the old man's head.

"I think that goes for all of us."

"Maybe he thought we were working for the secret police, for example."

"I doubt it," said Khaa'ina, adding, "there was this weird coldness in his expression when you were asking him questions."

Qaa'id: "Why would a Palestinian refuse to tell his story of the *Nakba*, of being sent into exile?"

Mutarjima: "It's a traumatic memory for him."

Khaa'in: "First of all, don't start throwing technical words around. Second, you're prettier than usual today. Third, what the hell does 'traumatic' mean?"

Qaa'id: "Let's stick to the topic—we're talking about the old man. 'Traumatic.' More than sixty years after the fact? That seems odd. We're Palestinian, and there are older people of his generation close to us who talk all the time about what happened."

Mutarjima: "In any case, where we're concerned, it's over—right?"

"Of course."

"Definitely."

"No question."

Naturally this was a lie in which all four were colluding. It wasn't over, it couldn't be over; the newshound instinct in each of them was ablaze with curiosity about the old man's story. This despite the fact that, when they left the eldest son's house after the meeting, they'd gone their separate ways without comment. Qaa'id went to Jordan Street, bought a coffee, and sat alone on the hill overlooking Baqa'a Refugee Camp. Khaa'ina went home and sat in front of the television with the volume turned low. Khaa'in went home and had sex with his wife. Mutarjima went to a bookstore and bought a map of historical Palestine; she took it back to her apartment and pored over it.

All of them were convinced of the validity of the work they were doing, and yet each of them secretly felt guilty when they recalled the old man's voice at the moment he shouted at them. The anger that had come pouring out of him couldn't be meaningless. It wasn't about Israel, for example, or the Arabs in general, or politics, or oppression, or the refugee camps. At that particular moment the old man had directed his abuse at them, the journalists themselves, as if they were the ones who had driven him from his village, stolen his house, and destroyed his life.

"We agree, then."

"Will there be anyone else at our meeting with the boss?"

"I don't think so."

The friends left the café, each of them at heart apprehensive about what was coming. Khaa'in, as he made his way home, pondered their predicament, looking for humor in the midst of the murk. And so it was that each of his colleagues, on arriving home, discovered that their WhatsApp group had a new name: "Motherfuckers."

2

THE GRANDSON COULDN'T GET KHAA'INA OUT OF HIS MIND. After the reporters left, he got out his phone and searched for the name of the newspaper and its employee directory, where he found her. He wrote down her full name, logged onto Facebook, and found her page. Thirty-four years old. Married. One child. She'd posted only one picture of herself, with her face turned to the side and partially concealed by her hair. There was also a picture of her little boy. She'd been aware, surely, of how he'd looked at her when he was introduced to her, and the way his attention had been drawn to her throughout the meeting. She'd been wearing a short black skirt with a blue blouse, and high heels with straps. She held herself calmly and spoke little during the meeting. It seemed that her particular role was to record what was said on her smart tablet. After his grandfather's outburst, when the reporters withdrew to the next room, the grandson had heard her talking to his father about what had happened. As the reporters were leaving, he wished he could catch up with her and have a word just with her. He was pleased with what his grandfather had done, but at the same time he felt he would have liked to apologize to her.

In the course of his thirty years, the only thing that had ever taken him away from his grandfather was women. An engineer, he moved from one company to another in Amman, turning down opportunities to work in the Gulf, so that he could stay near the old man. He maintained that he had two selves: the one that was attached to his grandfather, and the other buried between women's thighs. He'd told his family long since not to broach the subject of marriage with him, leaving his father to complain that his son was sullen, ill-tempered, and difficult, that he seemed scarcely human, except in the presence of his grandfather and with women. The grandson had few friends and no real hobbies, his life undefined, as well, by any particular ambition. He kept saying he didn't have time for anything that might take him away from his grandfather or from chasing women. It was odd that his grandfather and women had become like two sides of the same coin. The grandson told his grandfather, in detail, about his romantic life, and he told women, in detail, about his relationship with his grandfather. The old man was familiar with each and every one of his grandson's girlfriends: their names, their physical attributes, their images in photographs, where they were from, even what they smelled like. The grandson would sit with his grandfather and narrate minute accounts of a rendezvous, or a phone conversation, even a sexual encounter. When he lost his virginity, his grandfather was the first to know. Even though the grandfather was by nature conservative and religiously observant, he didn't rebuke his grandson for his unbridled pursuit of women; he merely cautioned him, repeatedly, against causing harm to any of his girlfriends.

"Don't hurt women, son. Sleep with them, fall in love with them, play around all you want as long as you do them no harm."

By the same token, the grandson never dated a woman without telling her about his grandfather. By the second or third date, the woman would know all about this special relationship that bound the young man to the old one, and if things became serious between him and the woman, she might be invited to meet the grandfather in person. On each of the few occasions when the grandson had gotten deeply involved with a woman, he'd brought her to the house and introduced her to his grandfather, after having first made it clear to her that she should ask him no questions. And each time, when the woman left, he would go straight to his grandfather and ask what he thought of her. Not infrequently, the grandson's girlfriends perceived the old man as an impediment, and many of them had told the grandson he spent more time talking about his grandfather than he did having real conversations with them. He'd canceled a good many dates because he was with his grandfather, and he was often late because he was seeing to the old man's meals. Busy with his grandfather, he sometimes forgot other commitments entirely. On one occasion, a girlfriend told him he should think seriously about dating his grandfather instead of her. Between the incomplete history that the old man represented and the incomplete presence that was the women in his life, the grandson could only keep searching for a fulfillment that seemed all but unattainable.

Many of his family members found his relationship with his grandfather baffling. In the grandson's boyhood and early youth, his father saw it as a natural bond between generations, regarding such alliances between grandparents and their grandchildren as a widespread and normal phenomenon. But their closeness increased with the passing years and grew deeper: all through the grandson's college years; after his graduation; during the ensuing job search; through brief periods of employment here and there and the stretches of unemployment in between. Sometimes the grandson slept in his grandfather's room. He would sit up with him, bathe him, listen to him, feed him, and take him places. All the while, the eldest son kept wondering whether his father had divulged his memories, his secrets, to the grandson. There had been many confrontations between the eldest son and the grandson concerning the grandfather's past. The father kept insisting that the grandson must know a great deal that he was concealing. The young man's denials were of no avail; his father remained unconvinced.

The fact was that he knew no more about his grandfather's history than his father did. As he began to mature and his awareness of the family dispute on the subject grew, he did try to use his close bond with his grandfather to break the wall of silence that the old man had erected around his past, but time after time his efforts failed. When he started at the university, his grandfather asked him to stop questioning him, and he acquiesced with a will, adopting his grandfather's position, and took to defending him against his father as well as anyone else who pestered him. Every year, on the anniversary of the *Nakba*, the grandfather brought his grandson a copy of the Qur'ān and asked him to swear on it never to interrogate any of his elders about what had happened to them that year. For all these reasons, Palestine, for the grandson, acquired the character of something like a legend: simultaneously real and unreal—something he saw every day without ever getting to know it fully, a mystifying text he didn't know how to read, despite its powerful effect on him.

Although the grandson had been brought fully over to his grandfather's way of thinking, he nonetheless never gave up hope that the old man would single him out in sharing something of his past, something that would confirm for him that he was unique in his grandfather's eyes. The grandson obeyed his grandfather's request to refrain from questioning him about his memories, but he kept waiting for some chance moment to come along, the one little thing that might induce the old man to uncloak the secrets he kept so tightly concealed. As the years

passed, with no such revelation forthcoming, the grandson began seeing his grandfather in dreams. He couldn't quite remember the first time
it had happened, but, starting with the fourth or fifth occurrence, this
manifestation began to take a particular form, the grandfather appearing more open and speaking in minute detail of his past. The dreams
started to resemble a daily serial, consisting of episodes arranged in
chronological sequence. In these dreams, the grandson was an audience of one, keeping a notebook in which he wrote down the old man's
stories, his anecdotes, those veiled recollections. In the beginning, the
grandson would awaken engulfed by guilty feelings, as if in his sleep he
had invaded his grandfather's memory, ravaged it in spite of himself,
and forced it into the open in a way that, when he was awake, his grandfather absolutely refused. To atone for the guilt that weighed on him, the
grandson decided not to write down his dreams, to keep no record of
them. If he could not censor the contents of his dreams, then at least he
could maintain control over his reality.

Often he would look at his grandfather and ask himself whether or
not a dream he'd had about him bore any relation to the truth. One
night he dreamed about scenes of the grandfather's departure from
his village in 1948, in which the grandfather was carrying some pieces
of furniture, a *kufiyyah,* and other things the grandson couldn't distinguish. A group of Zionist soldiers approached the grandfather and
kicked him in the stomach, causing him to fall and drop the articles of
furniture, but the grandson didn't see what happened to the *kufiyyah.*
His grandfather was moaning, as the soldiers beat him; there were bare
trees in the background. In the dream, the grandson wept, and when
he awoke his face was wet with tears. He got up, and found the old
man at prayer, so he went and stood near him until the ritual was completed. He embraced his grandfather and cried, the old man staring at
him, perplexed. The grandson asked him to show him his stomach, and
when he did so he knelt in front of him and kissed him there, murmuring indistinctly. His grandfather asked him what was going on, but he
didn't dare tell him about the dream. The grandson was afraid that, if
the old man knew what he'd been dreaming about, he'd ask him to stop
having those dreams, and to obey him; then, whether the dreams really
stopped or not, he would feel even guiltier than before. The grandson
wanted the dreams to belong to him alone, the only opening he had

through which he might sometimes slip into a world to which he was otherwise barred entry.

Strangely enough, during the same period in which the grandson began dreaming about his grandfather, he also dreamed for the first time about a young woman with whom he was trying to flirt. The first woman was followed by others on subsequent nights, but unlike the old man's appearance in dreams, these female apparitions didn't conform to any set order or pattern. Sometimes it seemed the grandson was aggressive with these women, while at other times he was gentle. Some of the dreams involved vigorous sex, others only phone conversations, and still others he couldn't remember at all when he woke up. The interesting thing about it was that, once the grandson took a fancy to a woman, sooner or later she turned up in one of his dreams. Whether or not he embarked on a relationship with the woman, he could be sure that before long he would encounter her in his sleep: before the start of a relationship, if there was one, or after it ended; while he was in love or after there had been a split; after confessing his feelings or while he was still in pursuit of the object of his fancy, which could go on for weeks—one way or another, the woman would make an appearance in his dreams. The grandson read a number of books on dreams. He read Freud, no less, without understanding very much, but he gathered that he couldn't confine the interpretation of his dreams within a single framework. They weren't always about the fulfillment of forbidden wishes, nor did he always dream either to recall something to memory or to forget something. He didn't always dream in order to find out more about something. He didn't, in the first place, choose what to dream about. The one certainty was that dreams would inevitably come to him, sooner or later, based on real life or departing from it—either way, they would come.

And that night—after the journalists had left, the old man's abuse ringing in their ears—when the grandson went to bed he saw Khaa'ina in a dream. When he woke up there was some sort of feeling in his heart, a sting, a disturbance, a craving.

3

THE MEETING WITH THE BOSS BEGAN IN A JOKING SPIRIT and ended on a note that was no joke at all, finding the team in a worse fix than before. As usual, Qaa'id spoke for the group. He explained the circumstances and the context surrounding the projected report, and then came to the meeting with the old man. The boss listened, shaking his head, but did not interrupt him. On hearing the word "Motherfuckers!" he laughed and began to clap. Khaa'in put his phone on his thigh and sent a WhatsApp message to the group: "What's he applauding for?" Mutarjima shot back, "Evidently he agrees with the old man's judgment of us." When Qaa'id had finished his narrative, the boss addressed the four of them, wanting to know each team member's take on the incident, and what was the first thing they did after the interview. He asked them to suggest what, if they could go back in time, they might add to the interview with the old man and what they might cut from it. He wanted to know whether here or there, in the moment itself, they felt they had erred in some way or omitted something crucial. The room fell silent for a few moments after each of them had responded. The boss asked whether they had any questions or comments. It seemed the meeting was all but over.

"All right, then. What now?"

The four of them exchanged glances. What did he mean, "What now?" What did the man want, exactly? Before going into the meeting, they had agreed that there were just two probable outcomes. One was that the boss would ask them to write an abridged version of what had happened, and with that the file on the old man would be closed; this was what they were hoping for. Alternatively, he might oblige them to make a second attempt to meet with the old man and persuade him to talk. At his paper the editor-in-chief enjoyed a fearsome reputation, being known for his hardheadedness, his bluntness, and his intolerance of even the smallest mistakes—this despite the praise he received for his ability to motivate his staff, his encouragement of offbeat stories, and his expansion of a liberal outlook at the paper. If he were to ask them to go back again and meet with the old man, they would not be able to refuse. Mutarjima, aware of the boss's appreciation for her linguistic skills and her active role at the paper, tried to bring a bit of her own influence to bear.

"I would suggest that one of us should write up what happened with the old man, so you have it on record, and submit it to you within three days."

"Good. And then what?"

"Then we submit a formal apology to the newspaper for having been unable to complete the article as planned."

"Good. And then what?"

"Then we close the file."

The boss's expression changed. They saw his eyes begin to bulge, a sure sign that he was in a state of suspension between thinking things over and flying into a rage. "Close the file?" he said. His voice rose, approaching a shout. Khaa'in grabbed his phone again and sent a message. "Goddamn you, Abir—this is your fault." The atmosphere in the room was like that in a court of law, with the accused waiting for the judge to pronounce the sentence. They didn't have to wait long.

"We've got a remarkable situation here: an old man, a Palestinian, visited by Palestinian journalists who want to hear his account of the *Nakba,* and not only does he refuse to speak to them—he calls them 'motherfuckers' and sends them packing. If you want to write *that* piece yourselves, and submit it to me, I have no objection. Otherwise, I'll turn the project over to another team, in which case you will be required to answer whatever requests they may have for more information on what happened. Any questions?"

No. Of course not. No one had foreseen this. They themselves, then, were to become the subject of the story, turning that evening's events into a curse that would dog their careers in journalism ever after. How foolish they'd been. They had thought the boss would let them carry on with their work in the usual way, and now it seemed they had handed him a golden opportunity at their own expense. Close the file? Goddamn the old man! It was essential that one of them gather the courage to say something before the moment passed, and ask the boss to reconsider his proposal. So Qaa'id spoke up, saying that the crux of the story the boss was asking for lay in the abuse to which the old man had subjected them, without which it would fall flat, but that of course they couldn't print the old man's words in the newspaper.

"No worries—we'll figure something out."

"Sir, you don't want to damage us, surely?"

"I'm just doing my job. Your story belongs to me now—you can't get around that."

"Will our full names be included?"

"We'll use your initials. But certainly it will be made clear that the four journalists in question work for this paper. The candor and self-criticism we demonstrate by printing the story will raise our standing considerably."

And what about our *standing? Our lives, our work, you son of a bitch? Our initials will be printed—and that's supposed to guarantee our anonymity. Beautiful. Why not include our pictures as well?*

"What do you see happening after that?"

"Who knows? We'll have to wait and find out. Any number of things could happen. There might not be any buzz at all, or your story might really grab readers' attention and you'll become the talk of the town . . . or maybe you'll lose your jobs, or . . ."

It was apparent that matters had slipped entirely from the team's grasp, but just then an idea came to Khaa'in. He requested the boss's permission to step outside for five minutes for a consultation with his colleagues. When they had gathered in the next room, Khaa'in proposed that they bring up the issue of Palestinian identity with the boss. The boss, he said, had no right to trade on Palestinian stories simply to make news and increase the paper's readership.

Qaa'id: "Listen here, you—it's thanks to you and your fuck buddy Abir that we're in this mess to begin with."

Khaa'in: "Now you're looking for a scapegoat. Let's stick with my suggestion."

"It's a worthless suggestion," Khaa'ina put in. "You want us to tell the boss that, as a Jordanian, he has no right to talk about Palestine?"

Khaa'in: "Something like that. We can threaten him with our resignation and a scandal into the bargain."

Khaa'ina: "Very nice. He'll add that to the report he plans to publish about us, only now he'll include our full names."

Qaa'id: "I don't understand how you can think of turning the whole thing from a problem with an article to an issue of Palestinians versus Jordanians. What kind of idiocy is this?"

Khaa'in: "I'm not talking about Palestinians versus Jordanians—not exactly. It's a question of a non-Palestinian who wants to exploit our cause."

Qaa'id: "And what about us? Weren't we setting out to exploit the Palestinian 'cause' by writing a story on the old man? Every son of a bitch on the planet wants to exploit our cause. You're just talking nonsense."

Khaa'in: "That's it, then. Let's write the report ourselves. That way at least we can have some control over how it's presented."

Mutarjima: "Look, why don't you just use sex to solve the problem."

Mutarjima had not missed her opportunity to provoke Khaa'in and punish him for all the times he'd goaded her. "You bring sex into everything," she added. "There must be some way to put that to use now."

Khaa'in: "I could lay you out on the table in front of the boss, and yank that stupid veil off your head, and . . ."

Mutarjima: "Or maybe you could offer that beautiful body of yours to the boss. I doubt he'd turn you down."

At this, Qaa'id stepped in, telling them to shut up and work out their issues about sex somewhere else. Silence fell once more. Qaa'id checked his watch and realized that they needed to get back to their meeting with the boss. As they prepared themselves to go back, he glanced around at them and asked quickly whether it would be all right if, once again, he spoke to the boss on behalf of the group. He would, he said, offer a proposal that had just occurred to him. They all nodded, and Qaa'id opened the boss's office door. He asked for the floor.

"We'd like to try again with the old man," he said.

"How do you propose to go about that?"

"We don't know yet. But give us two weeks."

"What difference is that going to make?"

"We can't guarantee anything, but we've got nothing to lose by giving it another try."

"On the contrary, you do have something to lose."

"And what's that?"

"If you fail again, then that will be a new chapter added to the whole episode."

"True."

"And the rest of you?"

"He's our spokesperson."

"Good. You've got two weeks."

"Then we're agreed, but we want a promise from you."

"And that is?"

"If we manage to pull off the interview this time, then we want you to promise to make no further reference to our having failed the first time."

"I can promise you that. Do you have a clear idea of what you're going to do now?"

"Actually, no, but never fear."

"I see. Everything's fine now, is it?"

"Well, we're going to try. In two weeks, you'll have an article on the old man and his memories."

"All right. Meeting adjourned."

"Thank you."

"Don't mention it."

They went, heads down, minds seething. The moment they were back in Qaa'id's office, Khaa'in gave him the finger. "You can take your proposal and stick it where the sun don't shine," he said. Qaa'id asked them to keep calm. He declared a confidence he almost actually felt that they would succeed this time. When they asked him what made him so sure, he replied that what they needed to do was talk to the eldest son and explain things to him. He told them he had no doubt that all of them were eager to know more about the old man, irrespective of any threat from the boss. They would talk to the eldest son, explain to him their desire to renew the attempt at a dialogue with his father if at all possible, or at least to know the reason for the old man's bizarre refusal of their overtures. Khaa'in suggested that Qaa'id and Mutarjima be assigned this task, and that Mutarjima should endeavor to make the most of her evident intimacy with God to get them out of the trouble that had befallen them. Mutarjima gave him a withering look. "You know," she told him, "you just wish you could get close enough to me to smell my perfume. In your dreams! I'd roll in shit first." Coming back to the subject at hand, Qaa'id argued that it would be better for Khaa'in to take the initiative, since that would introduce some variation to the original scenario, from the standpoint of the old man. Khaa'in agreed, on the condition that Mutarjima accompany him. Annoyed, she stuck her tongue out at him, a gesture of mingled capitulation and contempt. Khaa'ina, meanwhile, had something else on her mind.

4

THE GRANDSON AWOKE WITH A START FROM HIS DREAM. In it, Khaa'ina had come, looking just as she had when he saw her at the abortive interview with his grandfather. The events of the dream took place in a derelict shack, in semidarkness. He was sitting alone on a couch in the middle of the structure, glancing around, to the right and to the left, as if he was on the lookout for her. Very slowly, the door opened, and he heard her speaking from the threshold, asking whether she might come in. He wanted to know whether she was wearing the same outfit in which he'd seen her at his home. She told him to look and see for himself, but he said there wasn't enough light for him to see her properly. She wanted to turn on the light, but he said no. *Just tell me.* *Tell you what?* *Same skirt?* *Same skirt.* *Same blouse?* *Same blouse.* *Same body?* *Same body—I'm barefoot, though.* *Where are your shoes?* *I took them off at the door.* *Could you go back and put them on, please?* *This floor can't support high heels.* *But I can.* She went and put on her shoes. He heard the clicking of her heels as she approached once more. He took her gently by the hand and drew her down onto the couch. He knelt before her, reached down and began undoing the straps of her shoes, gazing into her eyes all the while. She told him to stop, but he didn't listen. She asked him whether he remembered her name. *I don't remember anything.* *What do you want from me?* *I want to draw you out through your eyes, pick you up in my arms, and go.* *And then what?* *Don't ask. I don't know—I don't want to know.* *But I want to know.* He put his hand over her mouth and felt her lips beneath his fingers. He drew nearer, kissed her, embraced her, kissed her again, and then wept. He felt profoundly frightened, on realizing that he was in love with her. He slipped his hand inside her blouse, but she pushed him away, saying, *Not yet.* *What does 'yet' mean?* *What do 'before' and 'after' mean—what does anything mean?* *Your problem is that you don't know anything.* *What do you want me to know?* *My name, at least.* *I'll learn it from your scent.* *That's not enough.* He entwined his fingers in her hair, brought its strands close to his nose, and became aware that he was getting an erection. He asked her why he wanted her so much, why he wanted to occupy her and never leave. She shouted in his face and pushed him away again. *You don't know what I'm feeling right now.* You *know nothing—nothing. That's a lie. I know everything.* At this she burst out laughing, stood up, and pointed toward the door. *And this—do you know who this is?* There was someone standing there, some-one whose features he couldn't distinguish. The person came in and turned on the light. The grandson looked again, and before him rose the figure of his grandfather, looking stunned. Overcome with embarrass-ment, the grandson went to his grandfather, who pushed him roughly away, knocking him to the floor. He got to his feet, and when he looked again the old man had turned his back and was making his way, little by little, out of the house. He wanted to go after him, but his feet wouldn't carry him. Hearing Khaa'ina's mocking laughter, he turned and looked at her. *What—do you know him? Have you ever known him?* **What busi-ness is it of yours? That's my grandfather. He's my grandfather, too. No! Liar! You're a thief—you're all thieves.** *And you're a fool. You're weak. You're so weak, you couldn't even face your grandfather, and you won't be able to face me, either.* Enraged, he advanced on her—he wanted to slap her, but she faced him down, evincing a strength he hadn't observed before, defiant, breathing hard. She accused him of cowardice. He low-ered his hand and looked at her again. The light now revealed her to him entirely, and he realized that he hadn't really gotten a good look at her body when he saw her in his father's house that afternoon. The waistband of her black skirt was straining, as if she was trying to pull in her stomach, which bulged a little at the navel. Seeing him staring at her waist, she took his hand and calmly placed it there, looking him in the eye. He felt he had never in his life desired a woman the way he desired her. **Enough—please, that's enough.** *What do you want?* **I want to know.** *Not yet.* **Why?** *Because you don't know.*

Only a few hours had elapsed between when the grandson first saw Khaa'ina at his home and when she turned up in his sleep, but it wasn't this that most alarmed him about the dream. It struck him as soon as he woke up that this was the first time in his life that his grandfather and a woman had both appeared in the same dream. In his dreams before this, the grandson had lived in two parallel universes, where his grandfather and his women had never converged. How had the old man entered last night's dream, and why? What had he wanted, why had he shoved his grandson, why had he disappeared, what had he been so angry about— *And how,* the grandson wondered, *am I to learn the answers to all these questions, and why is my grandfather asleep now, while I feel as though there's this hole opening up in my chest that I've got no way to fill?* He went to the kitchen, where he took a bottle of water from the refrigerator and drank the whole thing at once. His watch told him it was seven o'clock in the morning. The household was asleep, the old man himself snoring so loudly it was as if the grandson had been intended to hear it. He went back to his room and sat on the edge of the bed, thinking.

He got his phone out, went to Facebook, and opened to Khaa'ina's page. He looked at her picture, hoping to find that it was somehow different from the woman he'd seen in his dream. It wasn't a very good image, and yet he felt as though he could detect her scent. There was nothing unusual in Khaa'ina's having taken over his thoughts so quickly, for he had always loved and hated on sight, but for her to show up in a dream on the same day he first saw her, and together with his grandfather, no less? This was a new precedent, demanding careful consideration. He was confused as to what he should do, given his proclivity for throwing himself headlong after his desires. Khaa'ina might well be startled if he were to send her a friend request on Facebook, considering his behavior during the interview with the old man and how blatantly he had sneered at the journalists, standing like a watchdog beside his grandfather. Now he wished he had spoken to her or escorted her to her car. Revisiting the events of the day before, he wondered whether Khaa'ina had felt his eyes on her as she sat there in the room where everyone had gathered. He searched his memory for the sound of her voice, the way she moved, what she had done in the course of the meeting. Had she laughed? Commented? Inclined her body in one direction or another? What had she been doing, exactly, while her idiot colleague had put his questions to the old man? Had his grandfather looked at her? Had his father seen her? He tried to imagine a scenario in which Khaa'ina was the one who questioned his grandfather, but he quickly drove that thought from his mind.

After about half an hour of mulling things over from this angle and that, he did send Khaa'ina a Facebook friend request—and then immediately regretted it. He thought about canceling it, but that would look childish. He hadn't worked out precisely what he wanted from this woman; the one thing he was sure of was that he wanted to see her again. He remembered her in the flesh, then remembered her in his dream, and was utterly consumed with lust. He would concoct no fantasies of an affair with a married woman; at the moment all he sought was to see her again—no more than that. He went to work, attended company meetings, had lunch, drank coffee, completed three tasks assigned to him by his boss, and talked to his colleagues in the staff galley, all the while thinking of nothing but her. He checked his phone at least fifty times to see whether she had accepted his friend request. What if she wasn't active on Facebook? What if she paid no attention to friend requests—which doubtless she must receive by the dozen? When he went home, his grandfather noticed that he was troubled, and asked him what was wrong, but he didn't reply. He sat in his room with the door closed, and waited.

He knew what all this tension meant—he had experienced it many times before, and each time he had recognized his own susceptibility to the object of his obsession. Although as a rule he was not given to writing things down, he had once tried writing a piece entitled, "Your Eyes Are My Frailty," which he'd presented to a previous girlfriend and shared with some of his friends, who praised it. Frailty. He'd given a good deal of thought to this word—he couldn't remember the first time he'd heard it, but he'd looked it up in a dictionary. He had always associated it with love, had often been struck by the existence of the technical term in Arabic that referred to "osteoporosis," but was in fact "frailty" resulting from bone loss, when there was no corresponding term that in some technical way described frailty of the heart. What is fragile breaks easily; at this precise moment, he was so fragile that if Khaa'ina had appeared before him he might have choked her with his desire for her.

At ten o'clock that evening he logged onto Facebook, checked his notifications, and leapt from his bed, so jubilant it scared him. He gave little thought to the next step. Like a spellbound child, he opened Messenger and began sending messages, feeling, with the intensity of his lust in that moment, as though she was sitting there half-naked in his arms. By sheer good luck, Khaa'ina was there at her end of the communication.

"Hi."

"Hi."

"Can I see you?"

"Who are you?"

"You know who I am. I'm sure you do. Can I see you?"

"Why do you want to see me?"

"I don't know. I just do."

"What if I say no?"

"Can we meet tomorrow evening?"

"No."

"Fine—seven o'clock, then. Al-Luweibdeh's a good spot."

"Excuse me, I'm logging off now."

"I'll be waiting—don't be late."

The grandson was feeling, just then, as if he was the happiest man on the planet. The expression on Khaa'ina's face, if he could have seen it, would have been inscrutable to him just then, its meaning to become clear only later.

5

TWO DAYS OF THE GRACE PERIOD GRANTED BY THE EDITOR-IN-CHIEF passed, during which Khaa'in and Mutarjima had no success at arranging a meeting with the eldest son to present their case to him a second time. Having gotten the son's phone number from Abir, Khaa'in called him repeatedly, to no avail. The eldest son explained that there was nothing further to talk about where his father was concerned, and that he wouldn't agree to see the team again. Khaa'in asked him the reason for the old man's reaction, what had made him so angry, but the son declined to shed any new light on the matter. After several conversations, the son stopped answering his phone. Khaa'in asked Abir to intervene, but she, too, demurred, on the premise that the incident had caused embarrassment for her with the family. On the evening of the third day of the grace period, Khaa'in and Mutarjima met at a café in the al-Rasheed neighborhood to brainstorm the options before them. Mutarjima, who seemed more discouraged than Khaa'in, suggested that they notify the group that they'd failed to complete their task, and put an end to this nerve-wracking charade. Khaa'in reminded her that it was early days yet—it would be premature, he said, to declare that they had failed, although he agreed with her that they were in a difficult spot, since the eldest son was so uncooperative. Mutarjima opened WhatsApp and sent a message to the group, summarizing her and Khaa'in's efforts over the past three days. Qaa'id replied, saying they shouldn't despair, and that they would lose nothing by renewing the attempt. Khaa'in asked him whether it might make sense to try to get the eldest son's sympathy.

"What do you mean?"

"I mean by telling him frankly about the position we're in. That the story will be published in any case, and the nature of its contents depends on him and his family. They need to know that, whether they like it or not, they've became a part of the narrative."

"The difference is that their names won't appear without their consent. They set that condition from the beginning, and we agreed to it."

"We can get his sympathy, then. We'll explain that our professional futures are at stake unless his elderly father coughs up."

Khaa'in asked Mutarjima to call the eldest son on her phone. She did so, but got no answer. What if, she asked him, they went together, unannounced, to the eldest son's house, and knocked on the door? Would they be sent packing? Khaa'in didn't think much of the idea, but he couldn't come up with anything better. While they were mulling it over, Abir called Khaa'in and suggested that they wait for the eldest son the following morning outside the building where he worked in Gardens Street. She told Khaa'in the name and address of the company, and he asked her to find out the son's work schedule, and what time he usually arrived.

At eight o'clock the following morning, a white Hyundai parked in front of the Sedco Engineering firm, in a road branching off of Gardens Street. Khaa'in checked his watch, wondering why Mutarjima had not yet arrived. Although she had a car, Mutarjima preferred to take Uber to work, to spare herself the stress of driving during the morning rush hour. Khaa'in had offered to stop by her place and pick her up in his car, but she had declined. He called her at ten after eight, but she dismissed the call, as a signal that she was almost there. Two minutes later an Uber pulled up, and there she was. Khaa'in observed that companies shouldn't employ veiled women who would inevitably be late for work because it took them so long to get dressed. His repeated attacks on the veil, she replied, were nothing more than a defensive tactic to disguise his obsession with veiled women, and his dream of getting close to them. He laughed. Her comment, he said, implied that veils were provocative, and that this in turn meant that they did nothing to dampen men's lust, so what was the point?

"The point is that it pisses off jerks like you."

"You wear the *hijab* just to piss me off?"

"I don't think about you at all. By the way."

"Liar."

"Idiot."

For a moment, Mutarjima was tempted to turn around and go back the way she'd come, leaving Khaa'in to fend for himself, but just then they found themselves face-to-face with the eldest son, who was walking toward the entrance to his building.

The eldest son was startled by the unexpected sight of his two visitors at this early hour. Khaa'in requested five minutes of his time. He replied that he had nothing new to tell them, and that he wouldn't permit another meeting with the old man. Mutarjima asked whether they might sit down with him in his office, or anywhere else, so that he might hear what they had to say—and that it was important. The eldest son sighed, puffing out his cheeks with exasperation. He told them he regretted ever having let them into his house to see his father to begin with.

"Just five minutes."

"What's the point?"

"Are we going to talk about this here on the street?"

"That's right. Here on the street."

"All right, then. Listen, we're in a real bind on account of what happened."

"What's that got to do with me?"

"Come on, man, please—the newspaper's going to print a fully detailed account of the incident, including the abuse."

"You can't publish our names."

"But our own names will be exposed."

"And how is that my problem?"

"Look, we went to your house in the first place for a worthy cause—I don't see how you can deny that."

"Maybe so, but the subject is closed as far as we're concerned."

"Please listen. All we want is one more chance with your father. If we could get any information from him, even just a little, then we could complete the article, and the paper won't publish anything about the original interview, which would humiliate us."

"Impossible. You're not going to interview my father again. Please understand—it's over. Leave us alone."

"Okay, then, explain your father's reaction to us."

"Look, you two, that's enough. I have work to do."

"We didn't think you'd be so hardhearted."

"Think what you like. It doesn't matter to me."

The eldest son was out of breath when he entered his office. Some part of him had really wanted to help these reporters, but he'd managed to suppress that impulse entirely and not let his face betray any signs of sympathy. He wasn't going to try with his father, and even if he did, those people would never get anywhere with the old man. If there were a second go-round, he might really blow his top—it might not end with just foul language. He called Abir on his office phone and asked her to persuade her friends to leave him in peace. He sat down at his computer and opened a file containing pictures of his father. He put on some soothing music, to calm his nerves, and began to go through the pictures. He felt the sting of tears, realizing that his father was nearing death, and would take with him to the grave the secrets all the world's exertions could never pry loose from him. He pictured himself attending a mourning ritual and receiving condolences from guests on his father's death. He imagined friends of his father's in attendance, people he didn't know, and how they might start discussing details of his father's past as to which he himself knew nothing: *When, exactly, did your father leave his homeland?* **I don't know.** *Did he take anything with him from his house?* **I don't know.** *Who went with him?* **I don't know.** *Who . . . ?* **I don't know.** *What . . . ?* **I don't know. I don't know. I don't know.**

While the eldest son was in his office having an existential crisis over his father's silence, Khaa'in was sitting in his car, conferring with Mutarjima as to their next move. It appeared that all avenues really were blocked, their mortification in the pages of their paper just a matter of time. Mutarjima raised again her original suggestion that they show up unannounced at the home of the eldest son.

"They'll call the police, and we'll be tossed into the street."

"I don't think so."

"But look, didn't you see how fed up with us the eldest son got while he was talking to us? He couldn't get away fast enough."

"What about the grandson?"

"Oh, for God's sake—talk about setting ourselves up for abuse we don't deserve."

They were interrupted by Khaa'in's phone. It was Abir, asking what had happened. He told her, adding that he was still parked in front of the building with Mutarjima. They agreed to meet Abir for breakfast at Abboud Restaurant, which was nearby. Mutarjima called Qaa'id and asked him to make her excuses to the boss for their late arrival at the paper. In a tone half-serious and half-teasing, he told her that, while they were trying to ferret out the old man's story, they had better be looking for other jobs at the same time, since it seemed the scandal was inevitable.

Abir didn't think much of the idea of their just showing up at the eldest son's house. Khaa'in, adding olive oil to his hummus, said they* had no alternative at this point, and that he might find himself driven to extremes in order to extract information from the old man. Mutarjima asked Abir whether the old man was known within his family for being irascible and moody. Abir said no, that he was the sweetest person she'd ever known in her life. "I've never known him to swear at anyone, ever, until you all came along." Khaa'in said Abir was indebted to them, since now, thanks to them, she'd seen a hidden side of her great uncle's personality. Mutarjima glared at him. The one good thing about the coming spectacle, she said, was that it would puncture his arrogance. Reaching for a piece of falafel, Khaa'in said with a laugh that he'd just treat the scandal as one more aspect of his struggle as a Palestinian to find out the truth. Abir laughed a half-laugh, with a look at Khaa'in whose meaning he understood.

"Would it be possible for us to see the old man somewhere other than at home?"

Pleased with Mutarjima's question, Khaa'in wondered why the idea hadn't occurred to him before. Abir thought for a moment, then said, "The Friday prayer. That's it. I'm sure he still goes to the mosque on Fridays."

Khaa'in laughed and said that would be an excellent opportunity for Mutarjima to prove what her piety could achieve. She ignored this remark. She picked up her phone and sent a message to the group by WhatsApp: "Friday prayer."

6

KHAA'INA WASN'T ESPECIALLY SURPRISED when she saw the friend request on Facebook. During the visit to the family's home, the grandson's confusion in her presence had been obvious to her. It hadn't crossed her mind to make eye contact with him during the session, in light of the nature of their visit and what they'd hoped to accomplish by it, but she knew he was not her type. He struck her as phony, the way he tried to prove how close he was to his grandfather, and his overly stern delivery of instructions. He wasn't bad-looking, but she was put off by his sneering response to the group and their project. She smiled broadly on seeing the friend request, sensing that she had added an important card to her hand, but her mouth fell open in disbelief when he asked to see her the following day. She decided to amuse herself for a bit with the cheeky kid, which meant she would have to conceal this subplot from her colleagues. She got home the next evening at around six and didn't go out again.

The grandson went to Jabal al-Luweibdeh flustered and eager. When he parked at Paris Circle it was a quarter to seven. He sat in his car and waited. After twenty minutes, he checked Facebook, but there was nothing. Then he realized that he hadn't specified an exact place to meet. He sent her a message but she didn't respond. He decided to get out of his car and walk around a bit. He headed for the arts center, Darat al-Funun, and went in. He sat at an empty table and ordered coffee. There was a film screening across the courtyard, to which he paid no attention. He tried to deny his own distress, but it was no use. He cursed himself for approaching her so precipitately. Here she was, a married woman who had visited the family with her friends on a job with the media and made an impression on him, and so, heedless of his grandfather, he'd dreamt about her and asked her out. How could he have expected her even to accept his invitation? He ordered a second cup of coffee and lit a cigarette. All at once his phone rang, and then slipped from his hand when he tried to see who was calling. When he'd retrieved it, he saw his father's name on the screen. He didn't pick up the call, but he was overwhelmed with a sorrow, freighted with fear, that went beyond anything he'd yet experienced. In that moment, he knew he'd lost the battle with this woman before it ever began. He drank a third cup of coffee and lit another cigarette from the butt of the first. His father called again, and this time he answered. His father asked him to come home if possible, as his grandfather wanted a bath. His grandfather! He felt as though he was repressing an obscure sense of unease toward his grandfather, the awareness of it coalescing in his mind. "What's going on with me?" he wondered. He went to Facebook: nothing. Feeling weak in the knees, he realized that if she were to appear before him right then, he would kiss her feet. He asked for the check and left. Downcast, he headed for his car.

He reached his home in al-Rasheed at ten and went straight to his room. His father soon knocked on the door and came in. He scolded his son for his lateness, telling him his grandfather had been upset, because he didn't get his bath that evening. The grandson just stared at his father and shook his head. His father asked him what was bothering him, but he didn't reply. If he opened his mouth, he might say too much, and his father was no use to him as a confidant. Grumbling, his father went away.

The grandson threw himself on his bed and considered his next move. He logged onto Facebook and sent another message whose subtext was that he had nothing left to lose. He saw from the Facebook icons that Khaa'ina was there at the other end, and that she was reading his messages. Indeed she was, her face brightening: here was yet another madman inserting himself into her world, but this was a special sort of madman. He kept sending messages, one after another, one asking, another explaining, a third making avowals, a fourth betraying anger, then a fifth, and a sixth. Khaa'ina couldn't believe how worked up he was. She wondered whether he really meant the things he was saying in his messages. She stood before the mirror and gazed at herself. She was used to these relationships, these flirtations and flatteries, and she had no need of anyone to affirm her femininity, but the speed with which this thing was happening now unnerved her. She didn't answer any of his messages. He asked for her phone number. She turned off her phone, went back into the living room, and sat down next to her husband.

The grandson woke up the next day feeling anxious. Weary, he went to work. During his lunch break he decided to contact her via Messenger.

Once, twice, three times. He went back to his office. He logged onto Facebook on the computer and left it open all day as he completed his tasks on different pages. His office phone rang—it was his immediate supervisor. His cell phone rang—it was his mother. It rang again, and this time it was his father. It rang and rang, until it seemed to him that the whole world was conspiring with her against him, while the only ring he wanted to hear at this moment was forbidden to him. He was having a second adolescence at the age of nearly thirty. He left work at five, having told his supervisor that he would not be in the next day. He got home and began calling. After an hour, he noticed that he had called Khaa'ina on Messenger more than thirty times.

Khaa'ina was beginning to feel both irritated and alarmed by all this attention. He couldn't have fallen in love with her so quickly. What kind of fool was he? Was he trying to impress her? He'd failed. Pique her interest? Failed. Entice her? Failed. Get her to feel sorry for him? Failed. There was no way, she thought, that someone like this could have had any experience with relationships. She was forced to mute her phone when she was at home, although she was expecting one of her colleagues to contact her about the problem of the old man and his story. *Three days since the interview, and not a word from anyone, all of us behaving as if nothing had happened; meanwhile here's the grandson pursuing me, just when I've had just about enough of sex with men.*

She told her husband she wanted to take the car out for a bit, to shop for some things they needed. She picked up her phone, and was about to call Mutarjima, to fill her in on what the grandson was up to, but then she decided against it. Her phone rang again. She thought of deleting Facebook and Messenger from the phone, but there was something in her that held back this impulse. She went to a pharmacy and bought a bottle of Panadol, her phone ringing. She considered blocking him on Facebook, but once again she thought better of it. At bedtime, she received yet another message from him: "Please say something."

The grandson opened his eyes to the sound of his grandfather calling from the next room. Wearily, he got out of bed and headed for the bathroom. His grandfather was surprised to see him by the bathroom door, his hair unkempt. "Not going to work?" The grandson said no, went into the kitchen, and made coffee. He sat by himself at the table, not asking his grandfather to join him.

"Why don't you want to tell me what's going on?"

Why? You're asking me why, Grandpa? It's from you that we learned to keep silent, Grandpa. Did you even see her, the way I saw her? How could you have sworn at them in front of her, Grandpa? Why can't I tell you all this, Grandpa? He looked at the old man and told him he was merely exhausted, and that he'd taken a day off from work. Not wishing to give his grandfather any opening to prolong the conversation, he got up and went back to his room. There was something about which he hadn't yet made up his mind, an idea that had occurred to him the day before, but he was beginning to lean toward going ahead with it. He wanted to see her, whatever the cost. He threw on his clothes, and slipped out of the house. He got into his car, and drove off.

At ten o'clock he parked in front of the newspaper's headquarters, and there he sat, waiting. He'd brought along a large cup of coffee, a bottle of water, a sandwich, a phone charger that worked in the car, three newspapers, and a novel, and he swore he would not budge until he saw her come out of the building. He didn't know exactly what he would do then. Would he get out of the car and talk to her? Of course he would— otherwise, what was the point of all this? But what would he say? And what if she screamed at him, as he was expecting? Well, let her scream. He braced himself for the worst that might happen. He hadn't come here with much in the way of plans or calculations in mind. He had just one objective, and that was to see her. Was that so hard, for God's sake? An hour went by, then two hours, and he became aware of how hot the weather was. He got out of his car and walked around a little, then came back. He ate, read, waited, read, waited, struggled to stay awake, waited, fretted, waited. In his mind he reviled her, then confessed his love for her, then waited for her some more, then all but damned himself to hell, then got pissed off at everything, then pounded the steering wheel with his hands, then remembered his dream about her, then felt overpowered by lust, then said, "Come on, come out, release me from all this!"

When Khaa'ina came out of the building she was talking to Mutarjima about that evening's rendezvous at Gloria Jean's Café to discuss the upcoming meeting with the editor-in-chief. The grandson saw her from his car and covered his face with his hands. In the tidal wave of all he'd been going through, he had forgotten that she and her three friends all worked at the same place. What a fiasco it would be if those other two assholes came out, and all of them saw him sitting there in his car like an imbecile. *Hello there—let me introduce you to the guy— you all know who he is—who's been chasing after me for the past three days like a fifteen-year-old kid. **What?** Yes indeed, the grandson, right? Who stood there next to his grandfather, laughing at us.* Dismissing the whispers in his head for a few moments, he took his hands away from his face. Looking around, he saw Khaa'ina and Mutarjima behind his car, heading for another car parked a few meters away. He didn't know whether his heart was beating with anxiety, desire, alarm, or . . . goddamn this heart of his. He had everything to lose if he got out of the car now and went after them. The narrative would be transformed from a personal thing between him and Khaa'ina to another episode in the tale of the four reporters with the grandfather's family. He didn't want that. The sensible thing to do now was to retreat, since he had achieved his goal of seeing her, however fleetingly. *Just start the car and get out of here, you deluded fool—don't humiliate yourself.* He glanced in the mirror and saw Khaa'ina getting into a car next to Mutarjima. As the two young women started off and their car drew up alongside his, the grandson ducked his head. He forced himself to calm down, and waited five more minutes, then started his own car and went his way. He got home, feeling conflicted about what had happened—but at least he had seen her. Before he could sit down and meditate on the image of her that he retained, his mind blazed all at once with a question that hadn't occurred to him until this moment: *Did she see me?*

7

"COME TO MY OFFICE ASAP." It was Sunday morning, nine thirty by the clock, when Khaa'in sent this WhatsApp message to the group. There was an implicit agreement among them not to discuss their mission during work hours, but Khaa'in and Mutarjima wanted to explain their new plan for meeting the old man to the rest of the team. Khaa'ina arrived first, followed by Qaa'id and Mutarjima. Once they were all gathered around the table, Mutarjima spoke.

"These days the only time the old man goes out is for Friday prayer. A contingent of us—just the men, naturally—will go to the mosque he attends, approach him after prayer, and try to talk to him. Abir will call us Friday morning to confirm for us that he's gone out and to give us the name of the mosque where he prays; we'll be ready. Khaa'ina and I will wait in the car outside the mosque, to help deal with whatever may come up. If the old man agrees to talk, we'll have two options: the men can either stay with him inside the mosque and conduct the interview there, or else accompany him to some other place, in which case we'll catch up with you. What do you think?"

Qaa'id raised an eyebrow at Khaa'in, who nodded his agreement with the plan. Khaa'ina opened her bag, extracted her phone, and glanced at it. Khaa'in and Mutarjima waited for a clear response from the others, but were met by an eerie silence. "What's it going to be, guys?" Qaa'id was rubbing his hands together, as he scanned his colleagues. He cleared his throat, and suggested that, whether their idea was a paragon of brilliance or the height of stupidity, it would present enormous challenges. Khaa'ina pointed out that today was Sunday, which meant they were looking at losing the next five days by waiting until Friday.

"What's the date on Friday?"

"May 11th."

"So there will be four days left of the boss's grace period."

"Right."

"A big risk, obviously."

"This is the only solution, now that the eldest son has refused to talk to us."

"And what will we be doing while we wait for Friday?"

"Khaa'in will read a book on prayer and the proper way to perform it, so that he doesn't embarrass us in front of the old man."

They all laughed, including Khaa'in himself, who now shook his finger at Mutarjima and admonished her. "If this plan of yours fails, you're going to take off your *hijab*."

"And if it succeeds?"

"Then I'll think seriously about seducing you."

Before Mutarjima could parry his jab in this oft-repeated sparring match, Khaa'ina stood up and asked who normally went with the old man to the mosque.

The editor-in-chief passed by Khaa'in's office and observed, through the glass window, that the four team members were meeting. He knocked on the door and went in, catching the group off guard with his sudden appearance. He smiled, taking in their tense expressions, and asked whether the work was going all right. They all nodded. He reminded them what day it was and how many days were left of the grace period he'd granted them; no one commented, but they did request that he not keep reminding them of the deadline, if possible, before the stay of execution was up. Grudgingly, he agreed, but not without alluding to his lack of confidence in the success of their endeavor. Mutarjima, angry, demanded that he treat them in a professional manner, and remember their distinguished contributions to the paper over the years. The rest of the group was impressed with Mutarjima's boldness—she seemed extremely agitated, and they hoped matters wouldn't escalate.

"You know what your advantage is?" said the editor-in-chief. "Your advantage is that you're Palestinian, and I have a weakness for Palestinians." Khaa'in took this as an opportune moment for levity, to ease the tension in the room, so he quipped that he hoped to God to intensify the boss's weakness in the coming few days. Everyone laughed, but as the boss was about to leave, Qaa'id spoke up.

"Be honest," he said. "Do you want us to succeed?"

"No."

That one word, dry and harsh, startled them into all speaking at once.

"*Why?*"

"Because the story of your failure would make for a more interesting piece."

"Of course. Scandal sells."

"That's not what I meant. But just think—the story of you all with the old man, his outburst, your trying to come up with some way of getting a second interview, it's unique, unheard-of. A fantastic subject for a newspaper article."

"Excuse me," Khaa'ina snapped, "but we are not material for people's entertainment."

"But think about it. We have two potential articles. In one, an elderly Palestinian man talks about his memories of the *Nakba.* In the other, he refuses to be interviewed and he curses out the journalists, who then start coming up with schemes to pursue the guy and draw him out, get him to talk. It's perfectly clear that the first type of report is just a rehash—there are millions of Palestinians who've shared their experiences. What's new about that?"

"What's new is that this old man is the last surviving member of his family to have witnessed the *Nakba,* and the questions we were going to ask him were unusual. We—"

"All that's been done before, I assure you."

"Fine. Thank you for your opinion. We'll meet again after the grace period is up."

"If I were you all, I would hope that the old man keeps his mouth shut. It would set a new precedent in journalism."

"We get the message."

The editor-in-chief rose and took his leave of the group, smiling coldly. They glanced around at one another. Why was this happening to them? The concept had begun with the inspiration simply to publish a piece on the *Nakba,* and now, day by day, the project was driving them toward new levels of lunacy. Their boss, the prick, wanted to use them as bait for his readers; the old man chose silence; the eldest son was ghosting them; and as for the grandson, he wasn't an option. Meanwhile, time wasn't about to stop for them. If they couldn't make the old man talk, the paper would proceed with its damning report on them, after which they might well lose their jobs. Not about selling the paper? What a crock. The four journalists' humiliation would be the sensation of the season. Their anger flared—it was as if they were up against a question of their own survival. Were they really going to let a senile old man destroy their careers in journalism, careers they'd built brick-by-brick over the past several years?

When the boss had gone, Khaa'in suggested a brainstorming session for them to consider the probable scenarios that might develop when they ambushed the old man at the mosque on Friday. There were three main concerns that preoccupied them.

First, the old man would most likely be accompanied by his grandson, a point Abir would confirm on Friday morning. They needed to think of a way to divert the grandson's attention from his grandfather for a few minutes. Their task would be more difficult if they spoke to the grandfather in his grandson's presence, since the latter was "an insufferable son of a bitch," as Qaa'id put it. Khaa'in felt this was a simple matter, that it might be possible to get someone at the mosque to distract the grandson.

"Suggestions?"

Mutarjima raised the possibility of obtaining his phone number from somewhere and initiating a protracted conversation with him immediately after prayer, pretending that the call was from some official source.

"Good. Other ideas?"

"Abir could be useful to us."

"Are you sure Abir actually wants to help us?"

"Of course. We'll ask her for the names of some neighbors likely to be there at the mosque. Then maybe we could ask one of them to approach the grandson, and . . ."

"At any rate, we need more time to sketch out this scenario."

"In my view, a phone call to the grandson is safer."

"We'll see. Is there anything you'd like to add?" This was addressed to Khaa'ina, who raised her eyebrows, but said nothing.

Second—starting from the assumption that they would somehow manage to distract the grandson—fine: Khaa'in and Qaa'id would move in quickly on the old man. Qaa'id would have a tape recorder in his pocket, which he would turn on. They'd taken pictures of the old man at the first meeting, and they needed no more of those. They'd sit in front of him. Good. What would they say? The old man would remember them. Would he blow up at them? "At the mosque? Not likely." Would he raise the alarm? That was a slight possibility. They would ask him first of all to explain why he'd been so angry with them, and they would proceed from there, depending on his answer. It was hard to make any minute plan where this point was concerned, since the old man would be taken unawares. They needed to be ready for multiple scenarios—inevitably they would have to resort to improvisation. The essential thing was to get answers, no matter how basic or abridged, that would be helpful to them in finishing their article.

Third, they had to assume that the old man wouldn't talk. A strong probability, no denying it. How would they deal with him? What would their next move be? They would approach the old man on Friday, May 11, and if he didn't talk, that meant there would be four more days left of the grace period. Would they make still another attempt?

"Why don't we hold off on thinking about that until after Friday?"

"We don't have that luxury—time is too short."

"But maybe he'll talk on Friday, our worries will be over, and then we'll only have wasted time by making false assumptions about what would happen."

Mutarjima was inclined to think in terms of such assumptions, since she was the most pessimistic of all of them as to the endgame. Would they try again if the Friday plan failed?

"Absolutely," said Qaa'id. "We'll keep trying until the grace period is up. I don't know how or where, but that's what we'll do—we won't give up. Remember, the worst thing that can happen is that we fail, and therefore we'll do everything in our power to avoid that outcome."

They all agreed about that, even though it was unclear what they would do if the old man refused to talk on Friday.

Before the team left Khaa'in's office, Mutarjima asked whether they were going to do anything before Friday. Qaa'id thought that he and Khaa'in should rehearse possible scenarios for Friday, while Mutarjima and Khaa'ina would be tasked with considering what would happen next if the old man refused to talk.

"That's it?"

"Wait a moment—is what we're doing legal?"

"Legal? What do you mean?"

"What I mean is, we have a statement from the family authorizing us to conduct an interview with the old man at their home, and to use the material in a newspaper report. That project failed. Now we're talking about getting information from the guy at any cost, and by doing whatever it takes to bring the story to press. Is that legal? What if the eldest son finds out and sues us?"

Mutarjima's question seemed so logical that they were surprised it hadn't occurred to them sooner. Khaa'ina suggested that they not go down that new and tortuous road just yet. Qaa'id backed her up, since it seemed to him the family wouldn't refuse publication of any statements they managed to get out of the old man—otherwise, why allow them to go to the house in the first place? Khaa'in chimed in, reminding the team that they would not, after all, be forcing the old man to talk, and that the family surely wouldn't object to publication of anything he said voluntarily. Mutarjima was less than perfectly convinced, but she agreed that they shouldn't be digging up new issues that might complicate matters. They dispersed and went back to their own offices, trusting that things would turn around in the next few days, and that their story would not end with the old man's refusal to talk.

III

THE GRANDSON PARKED IN A SPACE BY AL-SHAREEF CAFÉ and got out of the car. As usual, the place was insanely crowded; at this time of the evening it was nearly impossible to find a table. His father had called that afternoon and told him he wanted to meet somewhere, not at home, to discuss something.

"Why not at home?"

"I don't want anyone to overhear us, especially your grandfather."

The grandson suggested they go downtown, but his father preferred to meet at a place near home. The grandson kept mulling over what his father might have in mind, wondering what this could be about, but he couldn't come up with an answer. It was unusual for his father to go out with him, just the two of them, to a café, and he never smoked *arghilah*. He hoped his father wasn't going to bring up any thorny issues. He was already in such mental turmoil—he couldn't take any more stress. Whatever this was about must have something to do with his grandfather. Otherwise, why had his father insisted on meeting away from the house? The old man usually retired for the night at eight o'clock, but he left the door to his room open and wouldn't allow anyone to close it. His routine was to get into bed, switch on his night-light, and then he might stay awake for hours. Since he didn't often snore, it was difficult to be sure whether he was awake or asleep.

Surveying the tables and the customers, the grandson spotted his father waiting for him in an inside section of the café. He greeted him and sat down. They both ordered Turkish coffee, and the grandson ordered an *arghilah*. He wasted no time about asking his father the reason for the meeting, and his father was startled to find him in such a hurry. The grandson explained that he was under enormous stress, saying nothing—naturally—about the reason. His father said that he'd noticed that something was up with him, and had thought about broaching the subject, but had found no suitable opportunity.

"I hope that's not the reason we're here."

"No, although I have no objection to hearing about what's been going on with you this week."

"I'd rather not talk about it if you don't mind."

"Of course, of course. You don't want to talk. No one in our house wants to talk; meanwhile, I'm the one who has to suffer the consequences of everyone else's silence."

The grandson was startled by his father's sharp tone, and he understood that the subject at hand had something to do with the reporters, their report, and his grandfather. For the first time in days, his face registered a genuine smile. His father gave him a puzzled look, but he waved his hand and apologized. He appeared to be smiling in spite of himself, and he was at pains to cover his face when he felt the smile verging on a guffaw. He wished he could tell his father what it was that amused him. He wished he could let his father know just how much affliction the reporters' visit had actually brought upon the household. What if he were to explain to him that his son—a strapping young man, an engineer—could scarcely sleep at night for thinking about a woman he'd seen at their house for less than half an hour, a woman his grandfather had reviled? What did his father want to hear? There was nothing to tell. *Out of nowhere, a woman suddenly appeared in our home, and in my dream, and in my heart, and now I'm as empty as a dry well, and all thanks to my grandfather.*

"Why are you smiling?"

"I just remembered something. Nothing to do with you. Sorry. Tell me what's on your mind. Why do you look so upset?"

"The reporters have called me repeatedly—then a few days ago two of them came to my workplace, and tried to talk to me, and . . ."

"Who came?" the grandson interrupted his father, leaping agitatedly to his feet. "Who came? Who came, Dad? Why didn't you tell me? Who came?"

"Quiet, you lunatic! Sit down—what are you doing? A man and a woman came. I don't remember their names."

Really, Dad? Really? You don't remember their names? What about their faces? Her face? Her breasts? Her legs? Her scent? Goddamn it all! He tried to calm himself down. Remembering the *hijab*, he asked whether it had been the veiled woman or the other one, and learned that it was the one with the *hijab*.

"And the man? Was it the guy who asked the questions?"

"No, the other one."

"What do they want?"

"They're asking for another meeting with your grandfather. Or begging, more like. They've gotten themselves into hot water with the editor-in-chief at their paper, and now they've got to submit the report they promised on your grandfather. If they don't, the story of their failure will be published in detail."

"How so? What about us?"

"Our names won't be mentioned, but the paper will lay out in detail that the assignment fell to four reporters who work there, and all their colleagues will know beyond any doubt the identities of the reporters in question. In short, they're asking for our help."

"What did you tell them?"

"I said no, of course. I don't want to put your grandfather through the same ordeal again. What happened the first time was quite enough."

His father spoke for a few more minutes, explaining that he would have liked to help the reporters, not only because he didn't want them to come to grief in their work on account of the family, but also because he would really have liked for their project to succeed. He wanted to know his father's history, too, even if it had to be mediated by strangers. But because he knew that his father would react at least as badly as he had the first time if he were to encounter the journalists again, he would not allow them access to him. What he wished, in essence, was that the journalists could obtain the information they were seeking without the old man's knowledge. "That's the reason I wanted to meet with you here, on your own."

"I don't follow you. What's all this got to do with me?"

"I asked you this question before, and now I'll ask it again: Do you know things about your grandfather that the rest of us don't?"

"No, I don't! Why won't you believe me?"

"Because, of all of us, you're the closest to him."

"Where his memories are concerned, there's no one who's close to my grandfather."

"Look, can you even begin to imagine how painful it would be not to know essential facts about your father? Do you see? Do you understand what will happen to me if your grandfather dies without having told us a single thing about his past? A part of me will die with him. I won't be able to forgive myself. And I'm afraid I won't forgive him, either. Don't you see?"

His father's voice had risen; he was red in the face, and there seemed to be tears gathering in his eyes. The grandson tried to soothe him. He swore a sacred oath that his grandfather had never confided information to him that he'd denied to everyone else. The father was quiet for a few moments. Then he grasped his son's shoulders and shook him.

"You can help me."

"How?"

"Ask your grandfather what happened during the *Nakba.*"

"I asked him a long time ago—more than once. He wouldn't tell me."

"I know, but I want you to try again. Get under his skin in that special way you have, and . . ."

"What 'special way,' Dad? Give me a break—for my grandfather, this subject is a closed book, and you know it. I could try to persuade him to meet with the reporters again if you want."

"No, he won't agree. You know what? I lied when I said the reporters mattered to me—they don't matter. Fuck the reporters. They can take their project and go to hell. What matters to me is to know, to *know.* They were just a means to an end—that is, to learn about your grandfather. Do you know what it means to have to resort to using people we don't even know in order to find out who my own father is?"

The meeting, essentially, accomplished nothing. The grandson refused to bring up the past or any questions about the *Nakba* with his grandfather, especially since he had stopped asking years ago, and no longer evinced any interest in the subject when they were together. The old man would have been mystified if his grandson tried to persuade him to talk, given that the grandson had often defied his father by defending his grandfather's point of view. The grandfather might suspect his grandson's motive, connecting it with the journalists' recent visit. Then the grandson would lose the thing his grandfather granted him that he valued above all else: his trust in him. At a loss, his father buried his face in his hands.

"What are we to do, then?"

"Let's just forget about it, Dad. It's not the first time Grandpa has refused to talk, and it may not be the last. Let's go on as if nothing had happened, and—as you said—the reporters and their project can go to hell."

Really? Granted, that's what his father had said. But for him to repeat those words? What was he supposed to say? "They can all go to hell . . . except for one of the women"? I want to make an exception for one of the women, Dad. Damn all of them to hell, but leave me this one, Dad. He'd felt his mind split in two as he spoke, half of him talking about *them*, the other thinking about *her. If only you'd told me sooner, Dad, that they'd started calling you again. Did she try as well?* His heart burned when he imagined her thinking about his family again over the past several days. He had tried to get close to her, while she and her friends were trying to get close to his grandfather. What a paradox.

His father glanced to the left and to the right, then gathered his things and stood up. "See you at home," he said. The grandson studied his father. Part of him was sympathetic, to be sure, especially since he knew how devotedly his father loved his grandfather, and that his intense desire to know his history, during and after the *Nakba*, sprang directly from this love. Often the grandson had sensed that his father was jealous of him because of the special treatment he received from his grandfather, and that he believed there could be no question that the old man must have revealed something of his secrets to the grandson to whom he was so close. The father simply could not believe that his son had no knowledge of the mysteries his grandfather concealed, and if the old man were to die without speaking, the father would continue in his belief that the grandson was keeping back the grandfather's story. But no sooner did the grandson begin to sympathize with his father than the other part of him came awake, the part that would support his grandfather's position to the end. What business of his father's was it to know things his grandfather considered private? *Would you tell me, Dad, if I asked you for details of your love life before you got married, or about confidential matters at work or with your friends or embarrassing incidents from your childhood, or . . . ? Why shouldn't we treat Grandpa the same way?* His father, the reporters, and everyone who came in contact with his grandfather, they all saw it as a matter of public record: that the old man's memories of the *Nakba* did not belong specially to him alone, but to all Palestinians. Bullshit. The grandfather saw this as an intimate concern, something private, and he didn't want anyone else getting near it. Why not respect the one unique thing left to him from his homeland?

The grandson paid the bill and left the café. He started toward his car, but then, seeing how pleasant the weather was, he changed his mind and decided to stroll around a bit in the neighborhood adjacent to Jordan University Street. He felt the need to be on his own and take some air. At first the streets were very quiet, as if empty of people, although it was still early evening. He lit a cigarette and started going back over the exchange with his father. So she was thinking about them—not of him, necessarily, but he was part of the family that was on her mind at the moment. Would this fact change the direction of his relationship with her? He laughed when the word "relationship" came into his mind. It had been ten days since the embarrassing episode he had set himself up for in front of her workplace, and he was still wondering whether she had seen him. Two days after that incident, he had resumed sending messages to her, but she had continued to ignore him, and he had few other ideas as to how he might get close to her. Over the last several days, whenever he left work he'd headed toward the street where the newspaper was headquartered, on the off chance he might catch a glimpse of her, and if he had extra time during his lunch break, he would eat at a restaurant near her workplace. Anyone who saw him might have found it odd, the way he kept turning his head to the right and the left, like an amped-up pendulum, watching out in all directions. He was always on the lookout: whenever he stopped at a light, or went into a shop or a restaurant, or sat in a café, or checked his phone, or heard a woman's voice behind him. From this brief experience, he came to understand how enormous Amman was, and how foolish he was, how weak—how he longed for her to appear before him now, share this cigarette with him, and set his mind at rest. What if she lived in one of these streets through which he was wandering? There was a good chance she did, especially since the newspaper was also on Jordan University Street. He was seized by a strange temptation to enter each of the buildings in front of him and start knocking on doors and asking for her. He tried to remember the make and color of her car, but then he realized that he'd scarcely seen it—he'd been too busy cowering and hiding his face, on the day he'd staked her out. The last time he'd tried to connect with her had been the night before, when he logged onto Facebook and went to her page. Strange that she hadn't blocked him. She completely ignored his messages, but she didn't block him. *What, exactly, do you want from me? Me, I want to inhale the air you breathe, your voice, your silence. What is it **you** want?* He wondered what it would take to get her attention, after everything he'd already lobbed at her. He'd shown his cards much too early, and now it had come to something more like begging, like pleading for mercy, than an exchange between adults. Might as well carry on, then.

"I know what you think of me. No doubt you're saying that I'm just a nutcase, delusional. Believe me, this has never happened to me before, and I don't know why it's happening now. I'd just like to know why you're ignoring me. Why? Why?"

When he'd woken up that morning and found no response from her to his message, he cursed her to himself, and cursed the day he'd laid eyes on her. Deep down, he felt that he had to give up this obsession soon, but what his father had said this evening presented new angles on the question, putting his dearest wish—to see her again—within reach. Immediately aware of the direction his mind was taking, he was ashamed of himself, and condemned his thoughts: No—no, he would not try to exploit his grandfather to achieve his own private ends . . . and yet . . . no. Impossible. *I want her desperately, but this is my grandfather . . . and yet, if I could persuade him to see them again . . . but no . . . but . . . that dream I had . . . that's what it is, then . . . her and my grandfather, her and my grandfather, her and my grandfather.* He closed his eyes, overcome with terror—and with hatred for her.

Arriving home late, he turned on the light in the living room. Everyone must be asleep. He passed by his grandfather's room, pausing at the door and listening stealthily. Could it be that his grandfather was awake? He tiptoed into the room and stood by the bed. There was no light. His grandfather's breaths came rapidly. He sat in a chair beside the bed, as if waiting for something. Why not tell his grandfather what was going on with him and this woman, and ask for his help? Remembering that outburst, he smiled. *Yes, Grandpa, that's right: the woman who was sitting right in front of you—oh, yeah,* right *in front of you. The one with the jet-black hair and the wide-set eyes. What's that? The dark one? Yes, her. What do you think, Grandpa?* The grandfather's breathing quickened, as if he'd heard. *Has a woman ever bewitched you the way she does me, Grandpa? I don't want to know anything about the* Nakba, *or about your life before or after. All I want is to know about your relationships with women. Open that chapter of your life to me, old man. Was my grandmother the first woman you ever took to bed? Women, the war, Palestine and Israel—all that upheaval you've been through. You were fifteen at the time of the* Nakba. *The books recount so many great love stories that took place during wars—tell me your own love story.*

The grandson's phone rang, startling him and cutting short his reverie. He snatched it from his pocket, silenced the ring, and left the room. When he returned, he peered once more at his grandfather, hoping he hadn't woken up. He was about to go to the kitchen when he heard his voice.

"Where are you going?"

"I'm sorry, Grandpa. My phone must have woken you."

"No problem. What time is it?"

"Eleven thirty."

"Why are you still up?"

"I just got home a little while ago. I'm heading to bed now."

"Did you want something? Why were you in my room?"

Oh, there are things I want, Grandpa, for sure. If only you could help me.

"No, nothing, Grandpa. I was just checking on you."

"You're not going to tell me what's bothering you? You haven't been yourself for a while now."

"Work's been stressful. Don't worry about it."

"No, it's not your job. You've been like this ever since those motherfuckers showed up."

The grandson felt his expression change. So his grandfather had noticed. Either that or he'd been completely transparent and the entire family was aware that he'd been in another world since the reporters' visit. This was the first time his grandfather had mentioned them to him since the day they came. He felt besieged, but he found a way out of answering.

"Go back to sleep, Grandpa. I'm tired—I need to rest."

"You don't want to talk, then. As you like, then. Don't worry about me. I fall asleep quickly."

I don't want to talk, Grandpa. I don't want to. How about that! I think you know someone else who refuses to talk. Just imagine—me, your grandson, and I don't want to talk. What's so strange about that? He went to his grandfather, kissed his hand and his brow. "Good night."

No sooner had he left his grandfather's room and headed for the living room than he heard the old man talking to himself. He went back and stood by the door again, positioning himself so that his grandfather wouldn't detect his presence. He strained toward the voice, listening intently. Interspersed with his grandfather's words came a plaintive moan.

"For fifty years people have been asking me the same questions. 'What happened to you? How did you get out? Why did you get out? Did you resist? Why didn't you resist? Where did you go? How many of you did they massacre? How did you feel? What do you remember?' The same questions, they never change. I was just a kid, now I'm on the brink of death, and the questions are the same as always. What do you want me to say? Listen up. It's my *Nakba,* not yours. Who are you all, anyway, that you have any right to know what happened to me? And what do you want to get out of it? What happened happened. Go fight, go liberate Palestine. Quit asking what happened."

The grandson sighed. His grandfather, hearing him, called to him. He went into the room but didn't speak. They gazed at each other for a long time. Then the grandson surprised himself by asking his grandfather what he would wish for if he could make a wish. "To die without being forced to tell anyone about 1948."

The grandson went to his room, his heart heavy with remorse. *No one's going to force you, Grandpa. That's a promise.* He sat down, got his phone out, and went to Khaa'ina's Facebook page. He thought about the irony of the situation in which he found himself—the joke was on him. He could compel her to talk to him if he were able to persuade his grandfather to talk to her. If he so much as flashed her a signal that his grandfather was ready to meet with them again, she and her friends would come running. But his grandfather was silent, she was silent, and the grandson was suspended there between the two silences. No, no way would he expose his grandfather to another incident. He wouldn't use him to satisfy his personal whims with this woman who had defeated him. He opened up Messenger, determined to send her an extremely formal message, apologizing for all his outpourings, and promising to leave her in peace. But instead of doing that, he found himself writing that he hoped to see her, even if only once, just for an hour, a minute, a moment, in order to explain to her all that had happened to him since he saw her, so she would know he wasn't crazy, wasn't trying to harass her—it was just that, in fact, he couldn't get her out of his head.

"THE GRANDSON? THE *GRANDSON*? YOU TRAITOR! Why didn't you say something sooner? Why? Here we are, wracking our brains for hours on end to come up with ways to get close to the old man, and meanwhile you've got his grandson eating out of your hand! Why have you kept quiet all this time?"

Mutarjima was clearly beside herself with anger, her voice rising as she challenged Khaa'ina. The two were meeting at Mutarjima's apartment in order to sketch out post-Friday scenarios, in the event the old man still refused to talk. Khaa'ina had decided to come clean to Mutarjima about the grandson's obsessive pursuit of her. She told her about his messages, and how relentlessly he'd been pursuing her ever since the interview with the old man. She reminded her about the car that had been parked in front of their workplace two weeks ago.

"When I told you to look, and laughed, you asked me why I was laughing, and I didn't answer."

"And? That was him?"

"Sure was."

"That's crazy!"

"I know."

"But why didn't you let us all know?"

"I don't know. Maybe I was afraid—suddenly I was a player in this bizarre drama, and I didn't know what to do about it."

"What's your take on the state he's in?"

"I'm not sure. Initially I thought he was just another idiot like all the rest of them, taking orders from his dick, but his persistence, and his tolerance for my totally ignoring him . . . that surprised me, especially considering that I'm also embedded in a whole other context—his grandfather, the article."

"So now what?"

Exactly. Now what? Khaa'ina had understood from the moment the grandson started to pursue her that she held a weapon that could be used to rescue the team from the straits into which they'd fallen, but she'd been waiting for a propitious moment, thinking to maximize the grandson's usefulness to them. In these past weeks, she had come close to answering some of his messages, and even to agreeing to let him see her. She had never in her life lacked for lovestruck admirers, never had to go looking for ways to satisfy herself and her vanity. This man didn't appeal to her, and yet she was afraid that, if she gave him an opening, she might enjoy the part she would then play in his drama so much she would actually get attached to him. *The old man refused to talk about the* Nakba, *he insulted us, and now here comes his grandson, on his knees before me, begging for some sign from me.* What was she to make of it all? When she'd seen him that day in his car trying to hide his face, she'd perceived that his infatuation with her, as conveyed in all those messages, was genuine. After that she'd expected him to quit chasing her, but his campaign only intensified, and his language grew more feverish. He contacted her on Messenger so frequently that she had to mute her phone. She took to glancing over her shoulder whenever she arrived at work or left it, for fear he might be following her. Once she opened Messenger and wrote, "What, exactly, do you want from me?" But she deleted this without sending it. Another time, she wrote, "So why wouldn't your grandfather talk?" But at the last second she stopped herself from sending that one, too.

She described her confusion to Mutarjima.

"You've got to make a choice. What's more important—your thing with the grandson, or ours with his grandfather?"

"I know. I don't want to seem selfish, but if I were to bring up the subject of the grandfather with him he might know I was trying to exploit him, and I'd lose him."

"So? You told me you weren't even attracted to him."

"Right—not as a man. What I can't resist is this fantasy of me that he's constructed."

"What a load of crap. Here we are in one camp, and you're in a different one."

"Look, haven't you ever been in love? We know nothing about your private life."

"In sha'allah, I'll tell you all about it after the story of our failure—not once but twice—to get to the old man appears in the paper."

Khaa'ina laughed uneasily, then grew serious. Since her marriage, she'd had her affairs, but had treated them as hedonistic indulgences with no bearing on the rest of her life: sex, passion, whatever. Little romances soon forgotten as she moved on to the next adventure. And on it went. She never accepted presents from her lovers or invitations to lavish dinners or any sort of quid pro quo. She was always careful to remain independent, a free woman who knew what she wanted and how to go after it, without regard for the conventions of the society to which she belonged. The moment she felt she was no longer getting what she wanted from an affair, she ended it. She exploited no man and allowed no man to exploit her. Any guilt she felt had to do with her betrayal of her husband, nothing more. The grandson, now, was something else: not a mere dalliance, but a means of achieving the goal she and her colleagues sought.

"Do you think I can use the grandson to get to his grandfather?"

"You've got to try. It could be the strongest card we hold—we can't not play it."

"But play it how?"

Mutarjima suggested they call Qaa'id and Khaa'in and invite them to come over as soon as they could in order to discuss this unforeseen development and to put the finishing touches on the Friday scenario. Khaa'ina reminded her that their stated task was to speculate as to what might happen after Friday if the old man wouldn't talk. Mutarjima replied that the emergence of her drama with the grandson would inevitably change the direction of their thinking, placing Khaa'ina in a central role in the events of the coming days.

Then Khaa'ina's phone buzzed. She extracted it from her bag and looked at it.

"It's him?"

"Sure is. On Messenger."

"Answer it."

"No."

"Answer it."

"And say what?"

"I don't know—just answer it."

"Look, for two weeks I haven't answered a single message. I'm not about to change that without a really good reason."

"Are you nuts? Just do it. Say, 'I want to see your grandfather an hour from now,' and he'll take you to his grandfather."

"Don't make me laugh. No. I won't do it."

The phone stopped buzzing, then went off again, and again, and again . . . and again. Khaa'ina put it down on the table and sat next to Mutarjima. The two of them stared at the phone as if they were mortally afraid of it. For her part, Khaa'ina worried that the grandson might do something stupid if she allowed a meeting between them. Why had it been her fate to get mixed up with this family of lunatics? When the doorbell rang, Khaa'ina started to shake.

"Don't open the door."

"Don't be silly. Wait here."

"Please, please don't get up—it could be him."

"No, you idiot, it's a pizza delivery!"

They took slices of pizza and ate them in silence. Mutarjima saw that not only was Khaa'ina incapable of thinking independently about how to handle the grandson, it seemed her nervousness might well have undesirable effects. She offered Khaa'ina a cup of coffee, but Khaa'ina waved it away.

"Listen, desperate times call for desperate measures. Come with me."

"Where?"

"Just come on."

"No. I can't deal with any more surprises. Tell me what you've got in mind."

"Let's stop by the eldest son's place."

"Are you out of your mind?"

"We won't go inside the building. We'll just wander around the neighborhood."

"What for?"

"To get you to break through this barrier you're stuck behind. You should have seen the look on your face when the doorbell rang—then you'd know what I mean."

"What good will it do to go to their neighborhood?"

Mutarjima explained that they would park in front of the building, then sit in some nearby café or other. She said she had a sort of feeling that they'd spot the grandson passing by. Khaa'ina refused. What

Mutarjima was suggesting would be reckless, she said, as well as pointless. Mutarjima held her ground.

"We'll sit there for an hour, no more. If you see him, and he sees you, then that's a message from you to him."

"But what's the point?"

"The point is to confuse him so thoroughly that he can't understand you, just as you're too confused now to be able to understand him."

"I don't understand anything anymore."

"Never mind. Look, the grandson thinks you're just acting as if you don't even know he exists, the way a beautiful woman does with men who chase after her. If he sees you, that will change the picture he's formed in his head."

"What good will that do us?"

"Then we take it up a notch. We use him to lure the grandfather."

"It's a big risk. Listen, I've insulted this guy by ignoring him, right? There's no guarantee how he'll react if he sees us, is there?"

"Oh, come on—he'll kiss the ground you walk on."

"Aha. You just proved that you've never been in a relationship with a man."

"Fine, whatever. How about you set aside your brilliant mind for now and, just this once, listen to your friend who's so ignorant about the art of love? We've got nothing to lose. We might even have something to gain."

Khaa'ina gave in, fighting back her terror. While she had to admit she did want to see the hapless grandson, the fact remained that this naïve approach was the last one any woman as experienced in the ways of men as she was would have considered. Oh, well. She organized her handbag and got herself ready.

"Have you got any perfume?"

"This isn't a romantic assignation you're going to, my dear."

"Just answer the question—I'm about at the end of my tether."

"In my room. Help yourself to whatever you like."

"Hang on a moment—should we tell the guys what we're up to?"

"No, let's not."

"But this could wreck tomorrow's plan for the Friday prayer."

"Or it could solve all our problems."

When they got to al-Rasheed, Khaa'ina drove up and down the street without locating a coffee shop near the family's building. Unsure what to do, she looked to Mutarjima for further instructions. Mutarjima pointed at Harir Hotel, not far from the al-Rasheed police station. Khaa'ina reminded her that they intended to sit in a café overlooking the street, so they could see who went by. Mutarjima thought the hotel was their best option, since it was close to where the family lived. She suggested they spend half an hour there. They could sit in the lobby and have coffee, then leave and take a stroll around the neighborhood. Maybe something would happen. Khaa'ina's first mistake, she now realized, had been to agree to go with Mutarjima to begin with, since now she felt compelled to go along with whatever Mutarjima proposed. She turned the car in the direction of the hotel and parked nearby; the clock said six thirty. Khaa'ina cut the engine. The two of them climbed out and set off like Thelma and Louise— except that in this case they were, in some sense, looking for a man instead of running away from one. They sat down in the hotel and ordered coffee. Khaa'ina pointed out the irony of the situation.

"I'm like him now," she said, "when he came and staked out the newspaper offices in his car two weeks ago."

"Good. I hope today he sees you and you see him: it'll balance the account and we can start from scratch."

"Seriously, though, tell me—have you ever been in a real relationship?"

"Is it just because of my *hijab* that you're asking?"

"Why do you always assume everyone's thinking about your *hijab*?"

"Because they are. The way most people deal with me is based on my *hijab*."

"So take it off and that will change."

"That's beautiful: spoken by a woman who claims to be independent."

"Let's not go off on a tangent and lose sight of what we came here for."

"You started it."

"You know how I feel about the *hijab,* and you also know that I respect you, regardless."

"It's an act, this respect of yours. You think the *hijab* is retrogressive and that your not wearing it means you're more evolved as a woman than I am."

"What do you care what I think? You're being consistent with your principles, which is all that matters."

"Women who don't wear the *hijab* have no idea of the pressure we're under. You enjoy more of the privileges accorded to men in this society than we do."

"Aha—so you're a victim, and I'm aligned with the patriarchy?"

The waiter brought their coffee just in time to prevent things from escalating. Mutarjima suggested they change the subject and talk about the grandson and his grandfather. Khaa'ina nodded, then immediately heard her phone start up again; she shuddered. But the screen showed her husband's name, so she got up and moved away to talk to him. When she returned a minute later, Mutarjima asked her whether her husband had ever suspected her in all these years. Khaa'ina laughed. Part of the reason she kept having affairs, she said, was that she was angry with her husband for never, so far, having discovered her infidelities.

"What about him? Have you ever caught him cheating on you?"

"No. He's a very straightforward sort of man. He believes in God, Palestine, the Right of Return, and me."

"How nice. What if he finds you out someday?"

"Then the sky will fall on him and he'll lose his homeland, all at once."

After half an hour, Khaa'ina called for the check. When she'd paid the bill they went out and walked around in front of the hotel. The street was quiet apart from some traffic. The sun was getting ready to set over Amman, and there was a refreshing chill in the air. The two young women presented a peculiar sight, proceeding in the direction of the police station, then turning around and walking back toward the hotel, passing it as they went toward the eldest son's building, then back once more to the hotel: the same circuit, over and over. Mutarjima, feeling as though they had begun to attract stares from the hotel employees, was beginning to lean toward returning, perforce, to the car.

"No, let's stay a bit longer."

"So you've changed your mind? How odd."

"You may be the one who started this venture, but I'm the one who'll finish it."

Mutarjima yielded to Khaa'ina's decision and walked on with her. Khaa'ina stopped in front of the hotel entrance and turned her back to it. She took out a pack of cigarettes she kept on hand for when she felt the need. She extracted two cigarettes, lit them both, and offered one to Mutarjima, who gave her a look of irritation, and declined the cigarette. "Whatever," said Khaa'ina. She leaned against the wall of the hotel as she smoked.

"Please, let's go," said Mutarjima. "We're making a spectacle of ourselves."

Ignoring her, Khaa'ina continued to smoke, avidly finishing the first cigarette, then what was left of the second. "Let's walk some more," she said.

In silence, they walked for ten more minutes, tracing the same route. The sun dropped out of sight. Mutarjima was sure the hotel employees were on the verge of coming over to question them about what they were doing there, behaving in such a suspicious manner.

"That's enough. Let's get out of here."

"All right. Let's go."

Mutarjima went to the passenger door and waited for Khaa'ina to unlock the car. Khaa'ina was about to get in, when she paused. In the window glass was the reflection of someone behind her. Mutarjima raised her eyebrows, and Khaa'ina, turning halfway around, found herself face-to-face with him. Mutarjima sat in the car and hid her face in her hands. The grandson stood rooted in place before Khaa'ina; she was likewise immobilized. He stared at her; she stared back at him. After a moment, Mutarjima uncovered her eyes to see what was going on. There they stood, facing each other. This silence was the last thing Mutarjima would have expected from a meeting between these two. Khaa'ina's back was to Mutarjima, her expression out of sight, but the grandson was in that moment entirely exposed to her scrutiny. She studied the grandson's features closely as he stood riveted before Khaa'ina, searching her mind for a word to describe his affect toward the woman in front of him. Love? Lust? Infatuation? Longing? Ardor? Passion? All of these? None? She wished she could see Khaa'ina's face as well, but she wasn't about to get out of the car. She felt herself admiring Khaa'ina for the terror she must have inspired in the grandson, considering how he was looking at her. The scene was frozen, its actors seemingly turned to stone. *What are they doing? What is all this about?* She thought about leaning on the horn, to put an end to this standoff and force Khaa'ina to get in the car. Then she came up with a simpler solution. She took out her phone and called Khaa'ina's number. At last Khaa'ina moved, seizing her phone and seeing Mutarjima's name. Stowing the phone in her pocket, she stood for a few more moments in front of the grandson, who still made no move. At last she turned away, got into the car beside her friend, and they drove off.

Back they went to Mutarjima's place. They had spoken not a word the whole way, which was not at all what Khaa'ina had expected. As soon as they were seated on the couch, Mutarjima called Qaa'id, and asked him to come right away, and to bring Khaa'in. There was an important matter to discuss in connection with the old man and their plan for the Friday prayer at the mosque. Next she turned to Khaa'ina.

"Are you going to say anything?"

"What do you want me to say?"

"What happened? Why didn't the two of you speak?"

"I couldn't do anything at all. It was as if I'd lost all power of movement and speech—I was paralyzed."

"Were you looking at him the way he was looking at you?"

"You didn't see me?"

"No, your back was turned. I could only see him."

"How was he looking at me?"

"Oh, come on! Are you actually getting a kick out of this charade? At the expense of our main objective."

"Just answer me. How was he looking at me?"

"Like someone who was about to cry."

"Really? I didn't notice that."

"What *did* you notice?"

"I thought he was going to kiss me."

"That would have been even more banal than tears. More naïve. He's smarter than you are."

"There are no smart men."

"Why didn't you take the initiative?"

"I felt as though, if I took his hand, he'd never let go of me."

Qaa'id called Mutarjima, told her they were two minutes away from her building, and asked her whether she needed anything. Khaa'ina asked Mutarjima to let her off the hook, not make her explain her saga with the grandson in detail, yet again, to Qaa'id and Khaa'in. Mutarjima suggested she leave as soon as the other two arrived and then come back after ten minutes.

Khaa'ina opened the door to their friends, and laughed when she saw that Khaa'in was holding a bouquet of flowers. "Where is the veiled enchantress?" he said. Khaa'ina excused herself, saying she was going out for a few minutes, and stepped aside. Mutarjima greeted Qaa'id, then turned to Khaa'in and told him to throw the flowers in the trash before he sat down.

"Why don't we sit in your bedroom?"

"You know what your problem is? Your problem is that you think you're amusing. The life of the party."

"Just admit that you're in love with me."

"I'd fall in love with my uncle's donkey first."

Qaa'id asked her why Khaa'ina had gone out. Mutarjima sat down and told them the whole story, including the face-off between Khaa'ina and the grandson earlier that evening. Qaa'id stood up, furious. Khaa'ina had no right, he said, to act on her own. "Calm down," said Mutarjima. As she saw it, she said, matters were evolving to their advantage, in spite of everything. Khaa'in called Khaa'ina, and asked her to come back. When she returned, she asked them not to question her about what had happened, but to confine their discussion to tomorrow's meeting with the grandfather. Grudgingly, the two men held their tongues, but Khaa'ina could see how angry they were.

"You could at least have let us know sooner about this relationship, given us a chance to think about how it might be useful to us."

"It's my own business, and I don't want anyone meddling in it."

"No, you do not have a monopoly on this 'business.' We're talking about the old man's grandson here, and it was thanks to our interview with the grandfather that he saw you in the first place. We're all part of this story."

"Everyone calm down, for heaven's sake," said Mutarjima. "What's done is done. Tomorrow is Friday, and we want to put an end to this nightmare. You two will go to the mosque and try to talk to the old man, while someone distracts the grandson—that's the plan."

"'Someone?!'" Khaa'in laughed. "I think we all know now who that 'someone' will be."

Khaa'ina could see there was no getting around her being the one to try to distract the grandson the following day if a major clash with her colleagues was to be averted.

"What do you guys suggest?"

·"Call the grandson as soon as prayer is over and talk to him for a few minutes."

"What if he's sitting right next to his grandfather while we talk?"

"I don't think so. He'll take the call outside the mosque, or he'll at least move away from the old man."

Qaa'id told her Abir had provided him with the grandson's phone number at the outset, when he was calling him to set up an interview with the grandfather. Mutarjima interjected that it would be better if Khaa'ina contacted the grandson via Messenger, because he didn't know her phone number, and he might not answer a call from a number he didn't recognize.

"Friends, whoever said the *hijab* veils the mind? Such sagacity!"

"If I weren't a collaborator in this enterprise, I'd be glad to see you fail tomorrow—fail and be publicly shamed . . . even though a mosque isn't the usual setting for such things."

Khaa'ina asked whether they'd established what, exactly, they were going to say to the grandfather.

Qaa'id stood up. "Actually, no. I figure once the grandson's out of the way, we'll move in, and we'll remind the old man who we are. I'll have a voice recorder hidden in my pocket, and I'll turn it on. We'll start with asking abridged versions of some of the same questions we asked the first time. If he won't talk, then we'll ask him at least to explain why. All we want from you is to keep the grandson busy for at least fifteen minutes."

Khaa'ina: "What if the grandson comes back and sees you with his grandfather?"

Qaa'id: "That's okay. If we've gotten the grandfather to talk, it won't matter. And if not, then it won't make things any worse."

Khaa'ina: "But then the grandson will know I tricked him."

Qaa'id: "No kidding—really? So you're saying we should care about his feelings?"

Khaa'ina: "You want to make a whore of me?"

"*Make* a whore of you?!" This was Khaa'in again. Khaa'ina got to her feet and reached over to slap him across the face, but at the last second he evaded her, chortling. Fuming, Khaa'ina spat on the floor, and started in on the subject of men.

"You *suck,* all of you! Men are the cause of all our miseries. From the grandfather, to his son, to the grandson, to our boss, to this scumbag here—if it hadn't been for his nonsense with Abir, we wouldn't even know this stupid family existed."

Khaa'in: "Fine. Rescue us then, mistress of love and soul of virtue that you are."

Khaa'ina: "If this interview were with an elderly Palestinian woman, in two hours she'd give us enough stories and reminiscences to fill volumes. This old man is setting himself against us as if we were trying to get nuclear secrets out of him. It's bullshit."

Mutarjima: "All right, that's enough, everyone. This isn't the time to start analyzing elderly Palestinians. We've come to an agreement, we're all set. I'll be with Khaa'ina outside the mosque, and we'll contact the grandson. It's you guys who have the most important role."

Khaa'in: "What do you say, on the occasion of this blessed agreement, you do us a special favor?"

Mutarjima: "What would that be?"

Khaa'in: "Take off your *hijab.*"

Mutarjima: "Have you ever heard anything so despicable?"

Qaa'id: "Look, man, I get why foreigners are obsessed with the *hijab,* but you're an Arab, a Muslim—you've been seeing *hijabs* since you were a child, you grew up surrounded by them. What's your problem?"

Khaa'in: "No, no—I'm not fascinated by the *hijab.* I'm only fascinated by *her hijab.* I think she's hiding some secret under it."

Mutarjima: "Yeah, I'm hiding secrets under it, all right. One of them is that you'll die before you ever see my hair."

Khaa'in: "What about your throat?"

Mutarjima: "I'd be happy to show you the spit inside it."

Unlike on previous occasions, no one was laughing at Khaa'in and Mutarjima's sparring. There was no mistaking the tension that had them all in its grip. Of all of them, Khaa'ina was the most anxious to see the conclusion of this drama, even if it meant nothing less than the end of the friendship shared by the group. Qaa'id was the first to leave, followed by Khaa'in. When Khaa'ina was on the threshold, Mutarjima stopped her and hugged her.

"Even if we fail in the end," she said, "and we're disgraced and we lose our jobs, you're going to be the only one who gets anything out of this."

"Yeah, I'll have acquired a new lover. Just what I needed."

"You idiot. Even *I* couldn't have resisted the way he was looking at you. How could *you*?"

IT WAS HALF AN HOUR BEFORE PRAYER TIME, and the grandson still wasn't ready to go. His father had roused him at ten o'clock that morning so that he could have breakfast with the family, but he had excused himself, saying he had no appetite. His father expected him to get up and get his grandfather ready for the mosque, but he begged off on this as well, asking his father to take over that task for today. His father was surprised at his recalcitrance, since he was normally so conscientious about tending to his grandfather's needs each Friday: bathing him, dressing him, and taking him to the prayer service. "All right then—what about the mosque? Are you going to ask to be let off of that, too?" The grandson assured his father that he would accompany his grandfather, but that he needed to be alone in his room until it was time to go to prayer.

On his way out, his father reminded him that his grandfather always liked to get to the mosque on Fridays before the imam ascended the pulpit. "I'm on it—he'll be there on time."

The eldest son closed the door, went to the living room, and told his father that he himself would see to him for the next two hours, until it was time to leave for the mosque. "Why? Where's your son?" The eldest son smiled, but made no reply.

What the eldest son didn't know was that the grandson hadn't slept a wink the night before. After his encounter with Khaa'ina and Mutarjima, he went straight home, retreated to his room, and stayed there. He lay in bed with the light off, eyes wide open, in disbelief at what had happened. She had come to his neighborhood, to his street, to his very self, and in spite of everything he had just stood there in front of her like a fool. No, it wasn't a coincidence. Her being there, along with her friend, in that place, could not have been unplanned. Was she looking for him, as he had been looking for her? But why? Why would she refuse even so much as to respond to his entreaties on Messenger, but then come to his neighborhood with her friend? Mutarjima had achieved her goal, for the grandson was thoroughly bewildered. He tried to come up with some rationale for the two women's appearance in the neighborhood as a matter of coincidence, unrelated to him. Had their car broken down? Had one of them had an errand at a nearby shop? Or needed to stop by the police station for some reason or other? Or been visiting a friend or relative? What could it be? *What? What was she doing on my street at that hour?* His head was spinning, and he felt as though he might choke. He'd been sitting on the balcony of the apartment when he caught sight of two women walking in the street below, on their way somewhere. He knew her even before he was able to get a good look at her face, which was in shadow because the sun had set. His heart was pounding, and, staring at them, he swallowed nervously. Leaving the apartment at a run, he charged down the stairs like a mad bull, raced out of the building, and scanned the street. The women were by the car, the same car he remembered from the previous occasion. He crossed the street and stood behind her. It took only a moment for him to realize that he'd lost his voice, and had no idea what to do, and by the time she had turned in a half circle and faced him, he was altogether at sea. No one would have believed him if he'd told them that she was wearing exactly the same clothes she'd had on in his dream. He heard a voice talking, inside himself. He heard himself say, "Hello." He imagined his hand, taking her hand. He imagined his lips telling her, as he took in her features fully, everything he had been through since he'd seen her. He imagined everything that might have happened but didn't. A minute went by, and they were still standing there facing each other like a pair of statues; he wished she would make some move. *Scream, slap me, tell me to stop chasing you, to forget you . . . I remember everything, I know every part of you, I've lived with you these past two weeks as no man has ever lived with you. Swear at me. Stop being you.* Nothing. *Blank upon blank upon blank, and here she is at last, right in front of you at last, her breasts, her thighs, at last, and her eloquent eyes, at last, the sky far away and she so close, her feet peeking out from her shoes, and here you are, totally emasculated, wondering in your heart when all this is going to end, when this woman will turn and go . . . this woman from who knows where, who knows how, who knows why . . . and is there a single word in the language to describe what I'm going through in this moment?*

After Khaa'ina and her friend left, the grandson had turned and gone back home. He was like an automaton, performing involuntary actions that made no sense to him. In his room, he thought and thought.

He picked up his phone and opened Messenger, wanting to contact her. Then he flung away his phone, cursing himself. He thought some more. It was midnight, and everyone was asleep; as dawn broke and the sun rose, everything looked faded and pale—like his heart, in which no one dwelt except her.

His father had left the room, but he didn't stir. He heard his grandfather calling him. He looked at the clock. He got out of bed, went to the bathroom, took a bath, got dressed, and went to his grandfather. He kissed the top of his head and apologized for not having performed the Friday rituals with him. Then he took him by the hand, and they left for the mosque. He asked the old man whether he would like to go by car. "No, let's walk." He adjusted his pace to his grandfather's labored steps without exchanging a word with the old man. In fifteen minutes they reached al-Rawda Mosque and went inside. The grandson brought a chair and settled his grandfather on it, then sat beside him on the floor. The imam ascended the pulpit, and greeted the worshippers. The muezzin gave the second call to prayer, and the sermon began.

The grandson continued to think about Khaa'ina as he listened to the sermon, which was about the virtue of patience in Islam. He imagined her sitting beside him. He imagined her in front of him, behind him, on top of him, and underneath him. Embarrassed by his own thoughts, he tried to drive her out of the mosque, but it was no use. The sermon continued, on the subject of patience in the face of trials and tribulations, a husband's patience, a wife's patience, the patience of parents, of workers, of students, of the poor, and all he wanted was for the man to stop, so he could ask him about patience in his condition, but he didn't know exactly what condition he was in, exactly, or what condition she was in—he didn't know her. How is it possible to be patient when you can't understand anything? The imam . . . patience . . . the mosque . . . his grandfather . . . He was not devout, and yet he feared God. *I beg you, come out of the inside of my head now. Wait for me outside the mosque.*

But of course she *was*, in fact, waiting for him outside the mosque. Khaa'ina and Mutarjima had arrived during the sermon and parked the car in the street opposite the mosque where they sat and waited. Mutarjima tried to break the silence that had settled upon them, but Khaa'ina wasn't up for chitchat. The two women heard the imam as he offered the closing prayers. When he reached the standard bit offering prayers for Palestine, Khaa'ina sighed. "What's the point of all this?" she said.

"What do you mean 'this'?"

"What we're doing. The old man, the report, the *Nakba,* and everything we're mixed up in."

"It's our job."

"Our job!"

"You're overthinking this. We can talk about whatever's on your mind once we've rung down the curtain on this drama."

Prayers were conducted and concluded; Mutarjima signaled to Khaa'ina. For several tense moments, Khaa'ina did nothing. Mutarjima reached over and poked her. Khaa'ina picked up her phone, opened Messenger, and glanced rapidly at the chat history between her and the grandson. "Come on," said Mutarjima, "what are you waiting for? The guys are in there—we have to make our move!" Khaa'ina pressed the icon, and the phone chirred.

Hearing his phone, the grandson hurried to take it out and mute it. Then he checked the screen. Turning to his grandfather, he told him he'd be right back. He went over to the shoe rack by the entrance to the mosque, put on his shoes, and went out into the courtyard of the mosque, only to find that the connection had been broken. He pressed the icon and heard someone pick up.

"Hello?"

"Hello."

"How are you?"

"Why are you contacting me?"

"Would you like me to hang up?"

"What were you doing in my neighborhood last night?"

"What are you talking about? I wasn't in your neighborhood."

"Look, I'm not crazy!"

"Really? You're not crazy? And how would you describe your behavior ever since you first saw me at your home?"

"Just answer me. Why were you hanging around my neighborhood?"

"I told you—I don't know what you're talking about."

"You were with your friend with the *hijab.*"

"It seems you're even crazier than I thought."

"Liar! I saw you with my own eyes!"

"Really? And what did you do then?"

"Don't play dumb."

"No, really—I'd like to know what you did when you saw me."

"You know very well."

"No, I don't know—tell me."

"I guess you have a right to make fun of me."

"Why? Did you do something awful when you supposedly saw me last night? What did you say to me? Did you tell me how in love with me you are? Did you hug me? Did you kiss me? Speak up—why are you suddenly quiet?"

"Stop it."

"You're saying that last night you saw the woman you've been endlessly harassing, begging her to answer you, to say just one word. So . . . what happened when you saw her?"

"Stop it."

"What happened?"

"Where are you now?"

"Why do you ask? You want to see me? You didn't get enough of seeing me last night?"

"Just tell me where you are."

"None of your business."

"I love you. I'm crazy about you, and I curse the day I first saw you. Please tell me where you are."

"Why? What are you going to do?"

"I want to see you."

"But you saw me last night, or so you claim."

"You know I'm not making it up."

"I swear I didn't see you last night."

"You're scared of me."

"Maybe so. You're nuts, you're a stalker—it's only logical that I should be scared of you."

"You know perfectly well I'm not a stalker."

"Oh, *no*, absolutely not. A stalker—*you*?"

"You've convinced yourself I am, because you're scared."

"Why am I scared of you, then?"

"You're afraid you might fall in love with me if you allow yourself to meet me."

"Don't play the role of ladies' man with me—that doesn't interest me."

"I'm crazy about you, and you know it, and you're afraid you might weaken if you get close to me, and that's why you keep avoiding me."

"Isn't it possible I'm avoiding you because you're a ridiculous, unattractive fool of a man, who means nothing to me? Hang up on me. Hang up, or I will."

"Wait."

"No, I'm not waiting."

"You know that, right from the beginning, I laid all my cards on the table. I was completely open about how I felt, how weak I was in my desire to see you. If all you want is to feel you've won—well, you did win, in the very first moment."

"Where are you right now?"

"At the mosque."

"Ha ha—oh, my God! That's a good one."

"I'm not joking. I'm at the mosque."

"May God accept your reverence."

"That's uncalled for. Don't mock me."

"You're talking to me while you're at the mosque?"

"I mean, I *was* at the mosque when you called, and then I went outside to talk to you."

"Aha. Nothing wrong with guys who stalk women going to the mosque to repent."

"This accusation of stalking is getting old. Tell me another one."

"The stalker apologizes to God for his actions instead of apologizing to the woman he stalked."

"Wow, you really have no imagination."

"Fine—maybe that will persuade you to quit chasing me."

"Why won't you admit that you saw me last night?"

"Because I *didn't* see you."

"Have it your way. Where are you now?"

"At the mosque."

"I can't believe I'm letting you ridicule me this way and I'm just putting up with it."

"What do you mean? Don't women go to the mosque on Fridays?"

"I can't imagine you ever go to the mosque yourself."

"Hey—I can be just as devout as you are. Maybe I'm trying to be a better person by imitating the lovestruck stalker who's obsessed with me."

"I'm not devout."

"No need to deny it—I wasn't making an accusation. You can be devout and a stalker at the same time."

"We don't have to drag religion into this conversation."

"Oh, right, I forgot—you're at the mosque. Okay then, you could be devout and at the same time helpless when it comes to me. That's a better way to put it."

"Do you pray?"

"No. Do you?"

"Only on Fridays."

"Why on Fridays?"

"Because I take my grandfather to the mosque."

"You've been talking to me all this time with your grandfather right next to you?"

"No, I left the mosque to talk to you."

"What did I do to deserve such an honor?"

"The trouble I'm having is that I can't tell when you're serious and when you're making fun of me."

All at once, the sound of indistinct shouting issued from the mosque. Looking over his shoulder, the grandson didn't see anything going on at the entrance, but even so he was unsettled.

"Listen, I have to hang up now."

"What's happened?"

"Nothing. But I've been away from my grandfather too long."

"Your voice has changed. Is something wrong?"

"No, no—I'll talk to you later."

Looking up from her phone, Khaa'ina studied Mutarjima for a reaction to what had just taken place. Mutarjima asked why the grandson had signed off, and Khaa'ina explained. Mutarjima was uneasy. The women were too far from the mosque to see what was going on there. Mutarjima tried to call Qaa'id and Khaa'in, but neither of them picked up. She suggested to Khaa'ina that they walk toward the mosque, but Khaa'ina said no, reminding her that it was essential that the grandson be given no reason to suspect that her conversation with him today was connected in any way to the men's presence inside the mosque.

They waited a few more minutes. Mutarjima made several more attempts to call Qaa'id and Khaa'in, to no avail. Moments later, Mutarjima sat up in alarm. She told Khaa'ina to look discreetly out the car window. She did, and there was the eldest son walking toward the mosque. There could no longer be any doubt that something bad was happening now inside the mosque, and that their two colleagues were in serious trouble. "Wait here for me," said Mutarjima.

"Where are you going?"

Ignoring Khaa'ina's question, Mutarjima got out of the car, crossed the street, and proceeded to the courtyard of the mosque, where she surveyed the scene. Aside from some produce vendors with their carts, there were very few people in the courtyard. Her heart in her mouth, she positioned herself beside one of the columns some distance from the entrance, but commanding a good view of it, while she herself kept out of sight. After about five minutes, she saw a group of people coming out of the mosque one by one. She peered intently, then saw Khaa'in and Qaa'id, who were being restrained by three men holding them from behind; they could not possibly have escaped. A moment later the grandson appeared, made for Qaa'id, kicked him in the stomach, and then rained blows on him, finally spitting in his face. Next he turned to Khaa'in, and dealt likewise with him. Mutarjima heard screaming and yelling, but nothing intelligible. She felt she might collapse from sheer terror. She had no idea what to do. She wanted to go back to the car, but her legs would not support her. Her phone rang—it was Khaa'ina, but she canceled the call. The mayhem before her was like something from a movie. She couldn't remember ever in her life having felt anything like the fear overtaking her at this moment. As she watched, the grandson made as if to resume his assault on Qaa'id and Khaa'in, but she saw his father intervene. The mob released the two men, who fell to the ground. The eldest son approached them, his lips moving. Then everyone except Khaa'in and Qaa'id went back into the mosque, leaving the two men lying in the dust outside. Mutarjima saw them struggling to rise. Having staggered to their feet, they went off in opposite directions, without exchanging a word.

Stunned, Mutarjima went back to the car, and got in beside Khaa'ina, who asked her what was wrong. No sooner was the question out of her mouth than Mutarjima threw her arms around Khaa'ina and burst into tears.

"What is it? Tell me."

Mutarjima, still weeping inconsolably, only mumbled, "Please, let's get out of here." Khaa'ina persisted with her questions, but Mutarjima would not answer them. "I'm begging you, start the car. I'll tell you everything when we get back to my place."

Khaa'ina gave way and started the engine. Back at the apartment, Mutarjima flung herself on the couch, took off her *hijab*, and asked Khaa'ina to get her a glass of water. Khaa'ina tried to call Qaa'id and Khaa'in, but neither one answered the phone. She turned to Mutarjima with her questions, but saw that she was drifting off to sleep, and soon her eyes were shut tight. Something terrible had certainly happened— but what? Various speculations wrestled one another in Khaa'ina's mind. There was a moment when she thought of contacting the grandson, but she quickly discarded this idea. She picked up her phone and looked for something to watch on YouTube while she waited for Mutarjima to wake up.

An hour passed, with Mutarjima snoring, Qaa'id and Khaa'in not answering her calls. Her need to know what had happened grew more urgent, until she couldn't stand it anymore. She went over to Mutarjima and shook her roughly.

"Wake up."

"Let me be for a bit."

"You've been sleeping for more than an hour. You have to talk to me. I'm not going to spend the day here in the midst of everyone's silence. Even the grandson, who's so infatuated with me, hasn't tried to contact me. So what happened?"

"We're in deep shit, all of us. That's what happened."

"No more riddles. Tell me."

So Mutarjima described in detail what she'd seen. Khaa'ina listened, expressionless, but as soon as Mutarjima had told her everything, she burst out laughing. Such a reaction was incomprehensible enough all by itself, but then she stood up and began a wild sort of dance, giggling all the while. Frowning, Mutarjima stared at her in consternation. It struck her that any man who would dare to fall in love with a woman like this was surely doomed. Khaa'ina went on dancing and laughing. She seized Mutarjima's hand and pulled, apparently trying to get her to join the dance. Mutarjima thrust her away violently, upsetting

Khaa'ina's balance. She fell. Mutarjima went over to her to apologize for knocking her over, but Khaa'ina kicked her in the leg. Mutarjima yelped and drove her foot into Khaa'ina's back. Khaa'ina leapt to her feet, grabbed Mutarjima by the hair, and slapped her. Mutarjima threw herself on Khaa'ina and they both went down, yelling and pummeling each other. Khaa'ina, who was physically stronger than her friend, managed to grab Mutarjima's arms and immobilize her, but then she felt the shock of Mutarjima's teeth closing on her hand. She shrieked at the top of her lungs, freed her hand with difficulty from Mutarjima's jaws, and retreated. Mutarjima ran to the kitchen and came back with a knife.

"What are you doing?"

"I'm going to kill you, you bitch."

"Your kind couldn't kill a chicken."

"You're a lower life form than a chicken."

"Your problem is that you're incapable of dealing with complex emotions. Maybe that's why men aren't interested in you."

"That's right. They're not interested in me. I've left them all free to fuck *you*, one after the other."

"See? If you were free, like me, you'd be able to comprehend the way I've been feeling."

"The most contemptible kind of woman in our society is the one who thinks she's liberated just because she drinks alcohol and sleeps around."

"Put down the knife."

"What's the matter? Are you scared?"

"I said put it down."

"Get out of my house. I want you out of my sight."

"I'm going. But put down the knife first."

Mutarjima set the knife down on a little table in the corner of the room, and the two women stood facing each other. Mutarjima was afraid the neighbors might have overheard the noise of their skirmish, but no one had knocked on her apartment door. Khaa'ina went and gathered up her things. Then she went over and stopped at arms' length from Mutarjima. Each seemed to be waiting for the other to say something to put a cap on this final scene of the day's outlandish events, but they were both too drained to be capable of further action or speech. Khaa'ina went to the door and opened it. She heard the sound of the knife being tossed into the sink; Mutarjima heard Khaa'ina's heels clicking toward the elevator. Khaa'ina got into her car. Mutarjima sat down on the couch and turned on the television. And, simultaneously, as if it had been choreographed, they both began to cry.

"WHY DID YOU GO OFF AND ABANDON ME? Where did you go? Why did you leave?"

Since he'd come home from the mosque the day before, the grandfather's questions had been ceaseless. He repeated them when the eldest son and the grandson brought him back after prayer, all through lunch, when they sat before the television in the evening, on his way to bed, and the moment he awoke in the morning, his tone plaintive, like one forsaken, like a lover mourning his beloved. The grandson, hanging his head all the while, said nothing. Throughout the previous day, in an effort to avoid all his family members, he'd gone out at noon and not come home until the middle of the night. He got out of bed in the morning and went straight to his father to ask whether there was anything he needed him to do that day, because he intended to be out until late.

"Why did you go and leave me yesterday?"

"Enough, Grandpa—let it go, please."

"No, it's not enough," his father interrupted him. "You've been avoiding your grandfather's questions since yesterday. I'd like to know, too. How could you disappear like that, leaving him alone? Just look what happened."

"I left him in God's house, Dad. Grandpa, you were in God's house, you were God's guest. I didn't abandon you in the street. Who could have foreseen what happened?"

"But why did you leave the mosque?"

"I didn't leave. I was right by the door, and when I heard the noise I went back. I got an important call that I had to take, and I didn't want to talk loudly inside the mosque."

An important call. A dream call. A call he'd been awaiting for a lifetime. And when it came, his grandfather was left exposed to abuse. He brooded on the dream he'd had in which his grandfather and Khaa'ina had appeared together. *This is what it meant, then. When she comes, my grandfather disappears. The grandfather I've always idealized.* He was consumed with rage—at himself, at what had happened, at Khaa'ina, and even at his grandfather. He sensed that his grandfather would be forever a presence in his story with this woman, and he thought of telling him about her, much as he'd been accustomed to tell him about other women he'd met. *Oh, Grandpa, if you knew that you were with her in my dream.* He'd been exultant while talking to her the day before. Despite the cruelty of her words, her mockery, her spitefulness, he'd been transported by euphoria unlike anything he'd ever known. He'd felt himself mere steps away from seeing her, but what happened instead was this foul ambush by the two bastards who had assailed his grandfather in the mosque. On hearing the uproar, he'd run to his grandfather, thinking of her all the while; he'd shouted, thinking of her; he'd reviled the two men, thinking of her; in his white-hot fury, he'd pounded the two of them, thinking of her. The one thing the grandson failed to think of, failed to question at all was: Why had Khaa'ina called him at this particular time?

"At any rate, there's something important I want to talk to you about. Then you can leave."

The eldest son sat down with the grandson in his room, and explained to him that he was thinking of calling the police. He emphasized his anxiety that these reporters might never stop pursuing the old man, his fear that the attempt might be repeated yet again. "After all the punishment they've been subjected to?" said the grandson. The eldest son replied that the scandal that lay in store for the reporters if they didn't obtain the grandfather's revelations might drive them to unimaginable extremes. The grandson downplayed the urgency of the situation and declared that he had been unconvinced to begin with that there was any question of a scandal. He cautioned his father against getting nervous or carried away, and declared his opposition to involving the police.

"What would we tell the police, anyway?"

"We could lodge a complaint against the newspaper itself."

"Dad, the police would summon Grandpa for a statement, and the whole thing would get out of hand. Let's not go there. I'll bash their heads in if they come near us again."

"If I had thought things would get to this point, I'd have kissed your grandfather's hand and begged him to sit with them and answer their questions, however minimally."

"No. The hell with them. My grandfather's not their guinea pig. It's over now—blood's been shed."

"I wish you hadn't lost your head yesterday. That scene was grotesque."

"I'll shove my foot up their asses if they mess with Grandpa again."

"If I were sure the police wouldn't take *you* in for questioning, I'd still be inclined to call them, but I'm afraid our complaint would backfire. Those clowns might lodge a grievance against us on grounds of assault."

The eldest son's apprehensions were right on the mark, for the prospect of police involvement was a question much on the minds of Khaa'in and Qaa'id when they met at Qaa'id's place on Saturday afternoon to discuss the previous day's misadventure. If the old man's family were wary of bringing in the police, though, Qaa'id and Khaa'in were likewise hesitant. Their anxiety arose from their concern that, once the police got into the act, it would become a matter of public record, thus finding its way inevitably to the newspaper and to the editor-in-chief, at which point the damage would be incalculable. The men were all too aware of their predicament. For one thing, the project that was to have culminated in a successful piece of reporting was now facing certain doom; for another, the two of them had suffered a gross insult, beyond any misfortune that had ever befallen either of them at any point in their lives, from boyhood on. Qaa'id made a cup of coffee for his friend and sat down beside him. He was spluttering with rage.

"The grandson."

"The grandson."

"What ill wind was it that blew this project our way? That miserable lowlife beats the shit out of us, and all we can do is watch him go at it."

"Our grace period is up in three days. I can scarcely believe it."

"Should we just declare the thing a failure and turn our efforts to finding some way of punishing that piece of shit?"

"Let's wait and see what the girls have to say. We're not the only ones caught in this snafu."

"Where are they, by the way?"

How strange, Qaa'id and Khaa'in both remarked, that Mutarjima and Khaa'ina had not contacted them at all the previous night, or today, either. Were they aware of what had happened? They had to have been outside the mosque, since, in accordance with the plan, the grandson had gone outside when he received a call. Qaa'id was apprehensive.

"Shouldn't curiosity have driven them to ask after us?"

"They tried right after the prayer. I saw that some calls had come in."

"Fine, but we didn't answer—and they didn't try again?"

"You're right."

"Should we put complete trust in the woman the grandson's in love with?"

"She hasn't done anything to make us doubt her."

"The grandson is certainly crazy about her. Look how he left his grandfather's side and went outside the moment she called him. But what's up with *her*?"

"I don't know, but it strikes me as unlikely that she'd sacrifice her career for the sake of a passing fancy."

Khaa'in suggested they use WhatsApp to invite the women to a meeting. Qaa'id agreed and sent a group message: "Good morning. We have to meet today. How about an hour from now?" Khaa'in replied immediately, but Mutarjima and Khaa'ina took longer to respond. Qaa'id called them but got no answer. He sent another message: "Hey, everyone—the grace period is up in three days. Where are you?"

Ten minutes later a message came in from Mutarjima. "Sorry— I didn't hear the phone. I'm fine with a meeting, but not at my place."

Qaa'id offered his own home for the rendezvous. A few minutes later, Khaa'ina wrote. "How about that, you two are still alive—so why haven't you been in touch all this time?"

Her message astonished Qaa'id and Khaa'in. "We're the ones who should be asking that question," Khaa'in replied. "Seriously—do you have any idea what happened to us?"

No one answered Khaa'in's message. "It's no use getting into finger-pointing on WhatsApp," Qaa'id put in. "Be at my house in an hour."

Everyone agreed. From the living room window, Qaa'id saw Mutarjima get out of a car. "She came on her own," he said. "That's odd."

Mutarjima came in and greeted the men. Khaa'in asked her why she and her friend had vanished on Friday. Mutarjima replied that she was not going to say anything until Khaa'ina arrived, or, "until *she* gets here," as she put it. The men sensed that something must have happened between the two women, and they wondered whether the grandson had anything to do with it. "I said I'm not talking until she gets here," was all Mutarjima would say.

Qaa'id called Khaa'ina and asked where she was. "I'll be there in ten minutes," she replied. "Traffic is bad."

When Khaa'ina arrived, she greeted Qaa'id and Khaa'in, but acted as if Mutarjima was not there. Qaa'id sized up the two of them and asked them what was going on. "None of your business," said Mutarjima. "You wouldn't get it, you have no idea how women relate to one another."

Qaa'id: "All right, so it's none of our business. Why did the two of you just evaporate on Friday? When we came out of the mosque we looked for you in the spot we'd agreed on, but . . ."

Mutarjima: "I saw everything, and I told her about it. We know what happened to you outside the mosque."

Khaa'in: "Aha—and you didn't call to check on us?"

Khaa'ina: "I called repeatedly, and you didn't answer. Nor, by the way, did you two try to find out whether we were all right. In any event, recriminations won't do any good now. It seems we've all decided not to talk to anyone about the past two days. Now tell me—why did they beat you up? What happened?"

"After prayers were over, we kept an eye on the old man while we waited for you to call his grandson. When we saw him leave, we were thrilled, thinking our plan had worked. We approached the grandfather and said, 'salaamu alaykum.' There weren't very many others in his row, which reassured us and made us feel confident about speaking to him in a normal voice. The moment he looked at us, he recognized us—the same horrible old man who'd refused to recall what happened to him during the *Nakba* had no trouble remembering *us*. He drew back the hand he'd extended for a handshake with us and started raising a hullabaloo. We were startled and stepped back a little, but he kept right on bellowing. We thought of beating a retreat, but a crowd was gathering around us. He continued to shout—thieves, he called us, trying to rob him. He started yelling for his grandson. We tried to laugh it off, so as to convey the impression that there was nothing serious in the old guy's accusations, but just as we were about to leave, two members of the congregation stopped us. They asked us what we'd stolen from the old man. We said the guy was out of his mind, we'd never laid a hand on him. People started asking the old man what he'd lost, and he said, 'Everything, everything.' A gentleman came up to us and advised us to give back what we'd taken.

"So we said, 'Look here, folks, we didn't steal anything. You can search us.' The old man went from yelling to crying. He said we'd taken advantage of his grandson's having gone outside in order to rob him, and that this wasn't the first time, but that we'd tried to steal from him before. His tears riled up the crowd, especially since the people near him knew him well. Some of them asked whether we'd seen the old man before. We could tell something bad was coming. We didn't know what would be worse, to lie or to tell the truth . . . but we said yes. Some of the congregants shoved us, while others said that, since we were in a mosque, everyone needed to respect the sanctity of the place. It got a lot noisier very fast, and we saw the grandson coming at a run from some way off.

"The old man, when he saw his grandson, yelled at him, 'Where were you, you beast? Look what's happened. These dogs want to rob me!' The grandson lost it. He lunged at us, but some people grabbed him at the last second. We tried to tell them our side of the story with the old guy, but it had become a no-win situation. More than fifty men surrounded us, most of them prepared to believe the old man. I asked them to let us go, but some of them advocated for calling the police on the grounds that this was a repeat offense, and that this time the assault had taken place in a mosque. Just when we thought the arrival of the grandson was the worst thing that could have happened, the eldest son showed up, and the noose tightened even more.

"'You!' he shouted. 'You again, you monsters? What do you devils want from my father?'"

"With that, the crowd needed no further evidence of our guilt. They grabbed us, restrained us, and led us outside, where the grandson beat the shit out of us."

Qaa'id finished speaking and no one said a word until finally Khaa'in said it was the two women's turn to tell their own story. They continued to insist that it was a private matter.

Khaa'in: "These two weeks, there's no such thing as 'private' and 'not-private' among us."

Khaa'ina: "Oh, yes there is. What concerns you two is that I talked to the grandson and distracted him, as we agreed. I'm very sorry about what happened to you."

Mutarjima: "So now what?"

The question that had dogged them these two weeks: "Now what?" The Friday plan had been a spectacular failure, and it appeared that any further attempt to approach the old man was out of the question. Their options were looking slim to nonexistent. The four of them sat in silence on the couch, each of them brooding upon their profession and their future as serious and respectable journalists who had built their careers from the ground up, until this business of the old man and the *Nakba* had come about, threatening to bring the whole edifice down on their heads. Khaa'in stood up. "What if we were to go see the boss tomorrow, before the end of the grace period, and submit our resignation?"

Mutarjima laughed. The boss would certainly accept their resignation, she said, but he might go ahead and publish a report on their failure all the same, and refuse to write letters of reference for them. That would mean they might find themselves sitting at home for months or even years.

They spent more than an hour talking intermittently. It became evident that they pinned their hopes on Mutarjima, by virtue of her being closest to the editor-in-chief and understanding how his mind worked better than the rest of them did. Qaa'id asked her whether she thought the boss really would publish the story of their failure if the grace period ended without their having succeeded in completing their mission.

"I'm not sure," she said. "Sometimes I feel as though he's not serious, and that he only wants to prod us into coming up with ways to make the project succeed. But we can't gamble on that."

Everyone noticed that Khaa'ina had contributed least to the discussion. Qaa'id now turned to her. "We'd like to hear your voice."

Khaa'ina: "I have an idea that might salvage whatever's left to be salvaged."

Qaa'id: "Okay, let's hear it."

Khaa'ina: "We won't try again with the old man, that much is clear. We've failed to write a report on the memories of a survivor of the *Nakba*. But why not change the topic to the old man's refusal to articulate his memories?"

Mutarjima: "That's pretty close to what the boss proposed."

Khaa'ina: "Not exactly. He wants to put our failure in the spotlight, and publish the story of what happened to us, in detail. But we'll suggest to him that any question of failure be set aside, and that the focus of the piece be on what might cause an elderly Palestinian to be so strangely and resolutely determined not to speak about his memories of the *Nakba*. We'll come up with a compelling title and publish the thing in installments. We absolutely won't go into detail about what happened between us and the old man. Rather we'll just say that he wouldn't talk to us, that he got angry, and turned abusive when he heard our questions. And we'll go from there."

Khaa'in: "I guess it could work, but it would depend on two things: the boss agreeing to the plan and the family's consent to the plan."

Khaa'ina: "Forget the family's consent. We won't mention any names. That way we're not obligated to get their permission. That just leaves the boss. What do you all think?"

Mutarjima: "Should we bring it up with him tomorrow, or at the end of the grace period?"

Khaa'in: "Tomorrow would be better, to give us time to think of other avenues in the event he says no."

Qaa'id: "There's one other thing. You say our report will concentrate on why the old man refused to discuss his past. How can we write about any such thing when we don't even *know* why? Why *did* he refuse, first of all?"

Mutarjima: "The unwillingness of victims to talk about the tragedies they've experienced is a well-known phenomenon."

Qaa'id: "We're not talking in generalities—we're talking about this case that's in front of us. We don't want this to turn into just our speculations. Why did he refuse, why did he get angry, why did he abuse us with foul language and turn our report into a nightmare from which we don't know how to extricate ourselves?"

Khaa'ina: "Because what happened to him is something private, and he doesn't want to tell anyone about it."

Qaa'id: "It's not private. Palestine belongs to all of us. His *Nakba* is part and parcel with our *Nakba*."

Khaa'ina: "There's no comparison. We've heard about it, but he lived it. Don't pretend to be a victim like him."

Qaa'id: "I'm not like him, but I don't understand his silence. There must be dozens of films and books that have recorded Palestinians' memories of the *Nakba*. How can we make the old man's reasoning plausible to readers of our report? For starters, are we going to defend him?"

Khaa'ina: "Of course we're going to defend him."

Khaa'in: "Bullshit. He has to talk, or at least he has to explain to us why he doesn't want to talk."

Khaa'ina: "He doesn't *have* to do anything. Did you look into his eyes when he was yelling at us? He doesn't have to do anything."

Mutarjima: "Given that the old man revealed nothing to us, our article, according to your proposal, will really constitute a general inquiry into victims' refusal to speak. I don't think any of us knows enough about this subject to cover it."

Qaa'id: "My sentiments exactly."

Khaa'ina: "Do you have any other ideas? Right now what we've got on the table is a report on our failure, the way the boss wants it, and a piece about victims' refusal to talk about their past. Which would you prefer?"

They all hung their heads, mute in the face of a choice that was no choice. There was truth in Khaa'ina's words, but Qaa'id wondered why she was so assiduously avoiding the subject of her relationship to the grandson. He tried to think of the best way to broach the subject without upsetting Khaa'ina, as had happened right before the incident at the mosque.

Qaa'id: "Did the grandson realize that there was a connection between your phone call to him and our presence at the mosque?"

Khaa'ina: "I don't know, but I have my doubts. He didn't try to call me again."

Qaa'id: "Could you . . ."

Khaa'ina: "Don't even go there. No, I couldn't. Enough about the grandson—please. That saga will end when our project with the paper ends."

Qaa'id: "Just listen. We want to know why the grandfather wouldn't talk. This would help us take the first step toward pursuing the option you yourself proposed."

Khaa'ina: "I won't do anything of the kind. If I so much as mentioned the old man, the grandson would connect all the dots and clam up just like his grandfather."

"You'd lose nothing in the attempt." This was Khaa'in. He was trying to hide his smile, but Khaa'ina was onto him.

Khaa'ina: "Look, the grandson means nothing to me. Neither does the grandfather, and for that matter neither do any of you. I just want to close this chapter with the least possible damage."

Qaa'id intervened. "All right, calm down," he said. Turning to Mutarjima, he said, "What do you think? Should we go with Khaa'ina's idea of writing about the grandfather's silence? We'd depute you to pitch the idea to the boss."

Mutarjima: "If we're all agreed on this plan, then I'll talk to him tomorrow morning."

They had their reservations, but, lacking alternatives, they agreed. Qaa'id apologized for not having offered them any refreshments, and asked them what they would like to drink, but Mutarjima said it was time she went home and got some work done. Khaa'ina followed her out and caught up with her at the building's main door.

"Wait."

"What is it?"

"I'm sorry about what happened."

"You just said we mean nothing to you."

"I'm under a lot of stress. I feel as if everyone's expecting something from me that I can't give."

"As I told you before, you're the only one who'll have gotten anything out of this debacle."

"I wish you'd just quit making these idiotic remarks already."

"Say what you like about me, but when the grandson calls you tonight, think seriously of asking him why his grandfather won't talk about his memories of the *Nakba*."

But the grandson did not call. She spent the whole evening clutching her phone, waiting. Whether or not she would in fact ask him about his grandfather she had no idea, but now—for the first time since the start of this whole disaster she actually wanted him to call. Perhaps she was hoping to reassure herself that the grandson had not connected their conversation the day before with Qaa'id and Khaa'in's presence at the mosque; or perhaps she wanted to be sure he didn't regard her phone call to him as having been responsible for what had happened to his grandfather; or maybe—the most disturbing possibility of all—she wanted to hear his voice telling her he was a broken man, even while she knew that she might not be able to hold out forever against such a confession.

IN THE MORNING, QAA'ID RAN FROM ONE TO ANOTHER of his colleagues at the newspaper. He was sweating profusely as he visited each of their offices to tell them the news: "The boss wants us right now." The clock read eight thirty. When they asked him the reason for the meeting, he replied, his words clipped, "I don't know, but there seems to be a problem. He was shouting at me over the phone." Via WhatsApp, Khaa'in asked his colleagues to stop by his office right away, before reporting to the editor-in-chief. Two minutes later they were with him.

"He's out of his mind. What does he want with us at eight thirty in the morning?

"It could be something unrelated to our project."

"No way. If that were the case, why would he have asked for all four of us?"

Up to now, they hadn't realized how frightened they were of the editor-in-chief. Each of them, with the exception of Mutarjima, harbored memories of bad experiences with him, but they would have acknowledged that their relationship with him was still founded on mutual respect. Qaa'id informed them that the boss had used the word "immediately" when he'd called ten minutes earlier, and just as they were about to leave Khaa'in's office, Qaa'id's phone rang. "It's him again. I'll put it on speaker."

"We're on our way," he said.

"So get your asses over here, already—where are you?"

Qaa'id swallowed nervously and glanced at the others.

"Excuse me, but why are you taking this tone with us?"

"Tone? You want to talk about tone? Wait till you get here."

The editor-in-chief hung up on Qaa'id. Khaa'in stared at his colleagues. "I don't want to go," he said. "I'm submitting my resignation right now."

Khaa'ina: "That won't do you any good. Our resignation seems like a moot point now, but he wants to see us. If he wants to see us, let him see us. Don't forget, we do have some rights here at the paper. We don't want to lose everything."

Khaa'in: "He has no right to abuse us. What did we do wrong, guys? How are we supposed to put up with all this psychological pressure we've been living under?"

Mutarjima: "Let's go see him now. That's our only option at the moment. It wouldn't do for him to have to come looking for us and for all the other employees to become witnesses to our humiliation."

Qaa'id: "I'm with you. Let's go."

Khaa'in: "As you all know, I'm usually the last one here to get bent out of shape. I'm the most cynical about everything, but I won't put up with being insulted. I'll throw my resignation in his face if he escalates this—I'll lay him out on the ground and trample him."

They left Khaa'in's office and made their way to the editor-in-chief. His office door was closed, and they heard a voice behind it that they couldn't identify. Mutarjima knocked.

"Come in."

They opened the door, and then all four stopped on the threshold, thunderstruck. "Come on in—what's the matter?"

Dumbfounded, they registered the presence of the eldest son, sitting opposite the editor-in-chief. They knew that the end of their employment at the newspaper really was upon them. They had hoped it would come quietly, but it was clear the boss hadn't summoned them for a chat, considering that he had been abusive on the phone with the eldest son right there in his office. Fantastic. How many times, in the space of less than a month, had the eldest son witnessed their humiliation? Who could even keep track? The eldest son rose. "I think I'm done here," he said to the editor-in-chief. "Thank you for your understanding." The editor-in-chief nodded, and the eldest son turned toward the door, where the four team members still stood rooted in place. He stared at them, his expression conveying equal parts anger and contempt. Qaa'id stood aside to make way for him as he left.

"Come in and shut the door."

The four of them stood in the middle of the room. The editor-in-chief got up out of his chair and began to pace back and forth, his hands in the pockets of his trousers. Then he stopped in the middle of the room, faced them full-on, and let fly.

"What the hell have you done, you morons? Imbeciles, lunatics, motherfuckers! For this you wanted a grace period, you maniacs? At the mosque, you pathetic losers? The *mosque*, you scumbags? You want to drag my paper through the public sewer, you lowlifes? Thirty years in journalism, and never have I seen stupidity like this. What rock did you crawl out from under? Have you ever actually completed a newspaper article before? How is it that you've worked at the paper all these years, you rats, you human filth . . . an old man, you dirtbags, and you wanted to force him to talk, eh? This is your idea of professional journalism? I'm ashamed of having put my trust in you, of having believed you were capable of acting responsibly."

His voice was loud enough to ensure that everyone at the paper heard him—no question. The team was caught flat-footed, with no plan for handling a scene like this. How had it escaped them that the family might contact their employer to report what had happened on Friday, as well as their pursuit of the family over the course of the past several days? They stared at their shoes and said nothing.

"So you won't talk, eh? Of course you won't talk. What *can* you say, assholes, after all the disgraceful things you've done, you fools, you . . ."

"Could you calm down a little?" Mutarjima didn't know how she had summoned the courage to interrupt him.

"Calm down? Calm down, yeah, I'll calm down, okay?" The editor-in-chief took a deep breath and drank some water. "I'll calm down—why not? It's perfectly simple. Do you know what would happen if this family filed a formal complaint against our paper? The complaint would be against the paper, ergo against me in particular. Can you grasp the magnitude of the scandal, the disastrous PR, the legal ramifications this would expose us to? And if the family were to take it to the media and give *them* the news? Oh my God. A Jordanian newspaper persecutes an elderly Palestinian man and incites a brawl with members of his family. These are the headlines, more details to follow. Journalists employed at a Jordanian paper took it upon themselves to persecute an elderly Palestinian man, and to assault him at the mosque after he'd refused to offer any revelations pertaining to his memories of the *Nakba*. Unbelievable. Details coming right up. And the old man's son had asked the four journalists, had implored them not to approach his father again, to leave him in peace. Great. What else? All this comes at the same time that Palestinians around the world are getting ready to observe the seventieth anniversary of the *Nakba*. Splendid. What a fine piece of journalism that'll make."

"If people knew the details of the story," Qaa'id interjected, "they'd sympathize with us."

Editor-in-chief: "Details? The details of a story in which an old man refused to talk. Full stop. The old man, the subject and object of the report, doesn't wish to make a statement. Full stop. What are we to do as respected journalists?"

Khaa'in: "We didn't 'assault' him at the mosque. That's a lie."

Editor-in-chief: "Lie or no lie, it will be viewed as assault."

"It was you who got us into this," said Mutarjima, trying to flip the narrative.

Editor-in-chief: "Ha ha! I knew that was coming. Pathetic weaklings like you always look for a scapegoat. And how so, oh esteemed journalist? Why should I shoulder the responsibility for your stupidity?"

Mutarjima: "You offered us a devil's bargain. Right after our first meeting with the old man, we asked you to close the book on this business and forget about it, but you threatened to publish the story of our failure—you wanted to make us into copy. And now look what's happened."

Editor-in-chief: "What's happened is that you're all fired. After today I don't want to see your faces."

"You can't do that!" Khaa'in exclaimed.

Editor-in-chief: "Oh, yes I can. If you knew the legal implications of what you've done, you'd understand that I could mop the floor with the lot of you if I wanted to. But I won't. Submit your resignations."

Khaa'in: "We won't keep quiet about this. We'll publish it with all the media."

Editor-in-chief: "See here. The old man's son was on his way to the police station. I was the one who persuaded him not to go. You have absolutely nothing in writing from me authorizing you to proceed as you did. All your foolish actions were your own idea. Yes, an inquiry could be opened, but we'd say that the journalists in question didn't consult us on their specific plans, and that we dismissed them as a consequence of their harassing an old man. If you want to go that route, so be it. You're individuals, we're an institution, and the institution will crush you. Listen to reason and submit your resignations. You'll lose your jobs, but you won't lose your careers. Now go."

Mutarjima: "But . . ."

Editor-in-chief: "No 'buts.' Immediate resignation, effective tomorrow, with payment of your salaries for this month. You won't have trouble finding other jobs."

Mutarjima: "What guarantee do we have that we won't be exposed even after we resign?"

Editor-in-chief: "I give you my word. And when I give my word, I stick to it—unlike some people."

Two hours later, the editor-in-chief had received notice of resignation from all of them. He asked them to clear out their offices within three hours and promised them that they would not be subjected to any nosing around or questioning by their colleagues. He sent an internal memorandum to the newspaper staff, announcing that these terminations had come at the request of the four employees themselves based on circumstances they did not wish to disclose. He also notified the Human Resources office to expedite the procedure, finalizing their benefits, tax arrangements, social security, and so forth. By four o'clock that afternoon, the four of them had been stripped of their identities as promising journalists at a distinguished newspaper and joined the ranks of the unemployed. Stupefied, reeling, they gathered in Qaa'id's office. How could this all have happened? "Did we really submit our resignations with our own hands?" It had started with an article on the *Nakba* and ended with a personal *nakba* visited upon their own careers. All their lives they had been ordinary Palestinians, seldom engaging in activism or demonstrations pertaining to Palestine. The *Nakba* and the *Naksa* and the whole Palestinian question were a part of their general context, to be sure, but this had not directly influenced the course of their private lives. Now, when they had gotten the chance to get closer, however superficially, to the issue of Palestine, they had lost their jobs.

"Just think what a huge cliché this is," Khaa'ina remarked. "It's Bollywood."

"Divine retribution, maybe," Khaa'in replied.

"Oh, spare me, please—retribution for what, exactly?"

"Do you know what the most ridiculous thing about this saga is?" said Mutarjima. No one replied. "The absurdity is that we took on a project, we got abused and insulted, we lost our jobs, and even now we still don't know why the old man wouldn't talk to us. He destroyed us by keeping silent, taunting us. He might as well have ridiculed us outright. Now I have this burning desire—and I want this even more than I want to have my job back—to know what his goddamn story is. To hell with this whole sorry ordeal."

Although everyone heartily agreed with Mutarjima, no one commented on her remarks. Khaa'in's phone rang, and he checked to see who the caller was before picking up. "It's Abir," he said. But when he answered the call he heard the eldest son's voice. He put the call on speaker.

"Listen here. I heard that you all resigned. I will regard this business as over and done with, and I won't take matters any further. But I swear to God that, if you try anything again with my father, you will absolutely regret it. Go look for other work and try to be more professional and respectful of others."

Khaa'in threw his phone at the wall, then ran over to it and stomped on it until the screen splintered. He turned to the group, breathing heavily.

"To hell with them and their progenitors. Only one thing matters to me right now, and that is to teach this fucking family a lesson. Especially the old guy—I'll show him the meaning of the *Nakba* he refuses to talk about."

Mutarjima turned on him. "Shame on you for speaking that way about the *Nakba*," she said. "Let's forget about Palestine for a minute and think about where we are right now."

Still furious and paying no attention to his colleague's rebuke, Khaa'in went on ranting in a manner wholly uncharacteristic of him in his colleagues' experience. "We've lost everything—we're defeated. But at least losers can afford to take risks because they no longer have anything to fear. Now it's time for revenge." It was scary, the way he was talking, the veins in his neck bulging as if he was in a wrestling match. "Revenge. This is me: the good-natured guy who never took anything too seriously, transformed in less than a month to a guy who's out for blood. I'll destroy them. I'll teach the old man how to talk. Oh, he'll talk, the old son of a bitch. Senile fucker—he'll talk all right. All of Palestine hangs on one side of the balance now—that old man's memories are on the other."

Mutarjima sat there trembling, thoroughly frightened. She hid her face in her hands, trying not to cry, but it was no use. She gave way to tears, with Khaa'in still bellowing his threats, while Qaa'id sat lost in thought, his head bowed, and Khaa'ina cursed the moment in which they had conceived this whole ill-fated venture. Qaa'id went to Mutarjima to soothe her, but she waved him away. He turned to his still-blustering colleague.

"Do you actually mean what you're saying?"

"Of course. Revenge. What else is there?"

"To achieve what end?"

"To get revenge. Don't you see what's become of us? Don't you get it that our lives have been destroyed in less than a month? I'm not just going to stand still with my hands tied."

"One more stupid move and we'll be in jail."

"Look, I'm getting my own back—with or without the rest of you, I'm getting revenge."

"We began this thing together, we'll end it together. And whether we go along with you or not, we're all implicated, where the family and the paper—and even Abir herself—are concerned."

"Okay, then. Let's get revenge."

"You talk about revenge the way you'd plan a walk in the park," Khaa'ina said. "Stop acting crazy."

"No, you listen to me. All my life I've hated myself for being a Palestinian, because it aligned me with a beaten people, unable to avenge themselves on the sons of bitches who robbed us and destroyed our lives. All my life I've striven for individual successes to compensate for the national defeat, which I take personally. I won't be beaten twice, not now."

Khaa'ina: "Perfect. This Palestinian identity you're talking about has driven you to crave revenge on a Palestinian family!"

Khaa'in: "I'd avenge myself on my own father if he screwed me over."

Khaa'ina: "All of a sudden you're a philosopher, thanks to this business."

Qaa'id: "Let's drop the sarcasm. Look, man, we're out on the street now, but we can still get out of this with minimal damage. What you're advocating, on the other hand, is madness, plain and simple."

Khaa'in: "One question—answer me truthfully. Don't all of you want to hear what the old man has to say about what he went through in the *Nakba*? Don't you want to know the secret that brought this clusterfuck down on our heads? I'll make him talk." He looked at each of them in turn. "Speak up. Don't you want that?" Mutarjima was dry-eyed now and a profound silence fell. When no one spoke, Khaa'in pressed on. "You do want it. I know you want it, just like me. And you know what? The old man wants to talk, too. He's just baiting us. Why not keep playing his game?"

Mutarjima stood up and at last joined the conversation. "Look, don't exploit our situation to vent your fury at the old man. We did what we did with the best of intentions and with appallingly evil consequences no one could have foreseen. How is attempting something criminal going to help?"

"Criminal? Who said anything about a crime? We'll make the old man talk. That's it—that's our revenge."

"How?" Mutarjima shouted. "*How?* For weeks we've laid plans and worked out strategies, we've begged the son and the grandson and Abir, the whole world, and it was no use. How? Tell me how? Just drop it. I'm sick of it, sick of it."

"We kidnap the grandson."

They all turned to Khaa'ina, gaping at her. They moved in closer.

"What did you say?"

"We kidnap the grandson."

"Come again?"

"We kidnap the grandson."

"Have you lost your mind?"

"We kidnap the grandson."

"But . . ."

"We kidnap the grandson. We kidnap the grandson, take him hostage to force his grandfather to talk. We warn the family that any attempt to involve the police will put the grandson's life at risk."

Mutarjima: "You're the one who compared this whole thing to a Bollywood film a little while ago! *Kidnapping?* Wow."

Qaa'id: "And you'll be the . . ."

Khaa'ina: "Yes, yes, of course I will. I know you're all surprised—I'm surprised myself. But there's no other way. We kidnap the grandson, with me as bait. Just help me work out the details."

Still her colleagues stared at her, aghast. So much for not committing a crime. What had happened to her? Previously she had vehemently refused to deceive the grandson or exploit whatever was between him and her; she'd barely agreed to make the phone call on Friday. Now she wanted to kidnap him?

Qaa'id: "Does this make you happy? Is this the sort of revenge you were after?"

Khaa'in: "To tell you the truth, kidnapping hadn't crossed my mind, but it's a good idea, and it's sure to succeed."

Mutarjima: "In that case, why not just kidnap the old man?"

Khaa'ina: "First of all, the old man wouldn't talk even if we kidnapped him, but for the sake of his grandson? Oh, yes. Second, it'll be easier to kidnap the grandson. There's no way to get near the old man, since he doesn't leave the house. Count on me and it'll all be over in an hour."

Qaa'id: "Let's meet in the evening and make a plan."

Khaa'ina: "No, no—no meeting, no planning. We've wasted enough time already. Tomorrow morning at nine o'clock I'll call the grandson and invite him to a rendezvous." She turned to Mutarjima. "I'll give him your address. We'll all be waiting for him, and when he arrives I'll sit with him for a bit. Then you all grab him from behind and do what needs to be done. We'll need to get some chloroform and a pad. Once he's out, we'll call his father and give him twenty-four hours to persuade the old man he has to talk about the *Nakba* if he wants to see his son again."

Mutarjima: "You watch a lot of movies, apparently. And you're volunteering my home to stage a kidnapping? Great."

Khaa'ina: "You know what? Being a translator really does suit you. Just a shadow. Your role is limited to providing commentary on what other people do. Meanwhile, you never actually take any risks, because you're scared of everything."

Mutarjima hurled a glass of water at Khaa'ina, but missed her target. Then she lunged at her, but Qaa'id restrained her, reminding her that they were still at the newspaper offices, and that they could settle their personal grievances after they'd put everything else behind them.

That evening Khaa'ina went home, went into her son's room, and kissed him. The maid told her that her husband had gone out a half hour earlier. On her way to the living room she asked the maid to get her a cup of coffee. Then she gave herself up to ruminations on the events of the day, and the idea of kidnapping the grandson. She hadn't intended any such intrigue, and even now she was shocked at herself. She would now play a role she had refused all her life to perform: that of the alluring woman who exploits her own attractiveness to entice men like insects into a Venus flytrap. But why? She was thoroughly baffled at finding herself so much at ease with this. She still chafed at her colleagues' evident expectation that she make strategic use of her connection to the grandson—and here she was, offering them just such a solution.

She lay back on the couch, opened Facebook on her phone, and brought up the grandson's page. She studied his picture as she went over in her mind what was going to happen the following day. She relaxed still more when she read his last message to her. Deep inside, in that remote region of her heart she kept scrupulously locked against the men who passed through her life, was a spur that had kept prodding her throughout the days just past, sharply cautioning her against allowing matters with the grandson to drag on, admonishing her that if he were admitted through the doorway into her life he would not easily be dislodged for reasons she both did and did not comprehend. While speaking to him on Friday, she'd felt enormous pleasure as he vacillated from one state to another: self-abasement, resistance, declarations of love. At that moment she would have liked him to know that she was no more than a few meters away from him, that she was in her car *and if only he would come and lay my heart bare, dismantle it piece by piece.* When he'd said he had to end the call, she'd been secretly upset. If only, she'd thought, a conversation like this could go on for hours on end. She nearly told him about the ambush that had been set up for his grandfather inside the mosque. Since she was accustomed to calling all the shots in her affairs, being the one who began them and ended them as she saw fit, she felt it was up to her to call a halt to the game with the grandson, but she'd been waiting for the deadline for submission of the report on the old man before taking any such step. *Now that the project is over, the newspaper is history, and everything's gone to pieces, you're going to get your comeuppance, my friend.* One call from her, and the grandson, his father, his grandfather, and all his tales of the *Nakba* would be in the palm of her hand, hers and her colleagues'. Is there anything more dangerous than a woman who knows exactly how beautiful and desirable she is?

IN THE MORNING, THE GRANDSON LEFT THE HOUSE EARLY, reaching his workplace at seven thirty. He went into his office, made himself a cup of coffee, and sat down to think. The offices were virtually empty, the place quiet as the grave. He couldn't believe what his father had said to him the day before: "Those no-good reporters resigned. All of them were mixed up in the mosque incident." All of them? *But Dad, how is that possible?* His father told him all about his meeting with the editor-in-chief, how the editor-in-chief had summoned the four journalists to his office with harsh words, and how the four had stopped short, flabbergasted, when they saw who was sitting there in the boss's office. The grandson questioned his father, trying to extract more information, but he didn't know anything more.

"How do you know that all of them were implicated in what happened at the mosque when the only ones we saw were the two guys?"

"I don't know. They may all have been involved in the planning, and the editor-in-chief treated them as a unit."

"But it's impossible."

"Impossible! Why?"

"I mean, the two women weren't there."

"Of course not, son—naturally the women weren't there in the mosque at prayer time, but they may have been waiting outside for their colleagues."

"Outside the mosque?" The color drained from the grandson's face.

"Right. I have no proof, but it's a guess, at any rate. By the way, you still haven't told me who it was that phoned you when you left the mosque to take the call."

Who called me, Dad? Who? Oh, my God, my God. He thumped his head against his desk. One of the company staff members noticed and came over to ask whether something was wrong. The grandson apologized and resumed his brooding. Did this make any sense? Ever since the conversation with his father the day before, he'd been burning with one question whose answer he wasn't sure he wanted to know: Had she actually called him in order to lure him out of the mosque and separate him from his grandfather? *Oh, my God.* Why had this not occurred to him sooner? Was there any other explanation? *Please, please, please, God, let there be another explanation. Could it have been a coincidence? Anything is possible. I'll drink fifty cups of coffee to convince myself that . . . oh, my God, a coincidence . . . She called me by coincidence, for the first time, and coincidence dictated that she should choose prayer time . . . It was a coincidence that my grandfather was with me, a coincidence that her two friends were in the mosque, coincidence that she hasn't talked to me since, coincidence that she'd been in my neighborhood the night before, coincidence that she appeared in a dream with my grandfather, coincidence, goddamn me and my heart and my body—coincidence.* He asked himself why he had come to work today in such a state—but then, he'd wanted to get away from the house. He hadn't left his grandfather's side since his father told him about the journalists' resignation the day before. He'd stayed close by him throughout the night, and when his grandfather wanted to go to sleep, the grandson had asked permission to sleep next to him. The old man was puzzled by his grandson's request, but he agreed. The grandson waited until his grandfather fell into a deep sleep, then hugged him and began to weep silently. His face was bathed in tears, and he knew precisely the source of his pain. For, in spite of everything, in spite of what had happened to his grandfather, in spite of the deception that had been worked on him, still he longed for her.

At about eight thirty, the company employees began to arrive. Some of them noted his unsettled demeanor, and asked him what was wrong. "Nothing." A colleague who sat next to him reminded him about the morning meeting that had been scheduled to discuss the company's current project.

They made their way to the conference room, the director arrived, and discussion commenced. Ten minutes into the meeting, one of the workers knocked on the door and said the grandson had left his phone on his desk, and that ten calls had come in, one after another. The grandson took his phone from the worker, apologized to the director, and stowed the device in his pocket. The director continued talking until he was interrupted by another call for the grandson. "Again? Would you mind turning off your phone?" The grandson checked caller ID, and his face changed. He asked the director for permission to leave the room for a few minutes, but the man refused, saying that, although it was only a short meeting, it could not be postponed.

"Excuse me, I have to go—it's an emergency." He didn't wait to hear the director's reply to this but grabbed his laptop and his suit jacket and hurried out, making for the main door. He called the elevator, and in two minutes he was in the street. He pulled his phone from his pocket and placed the call.

"Hello."

"Why did you do that?"

"Why did I do what?"

"I didn't think you were capable of such disgusting behavior."

"Look, I won't stand for being insulted."

"I'm not surprised that a woman would make fun of a man she knows is mad about her, but I never would have imagined you'd use me to get to my grandfather."

Khaa'ina realized then that she had, indeed, lost everything. She clenched her jaw and closed her eyes. So he was aware of how all the strands had been woven together. *Unfortunately, my friend, there is one last plot, and we'll see whether your infatuation with me blinds you to it. One last time, I will take you down, and in the process save myself from further entanglement with you.*

"I don't know what you're talking about."

"Of course. You don't know anything. After everything you did, you don't know anything."

"Let's talk face-to-face."

"I don't want to see you."

"Oh yes you do. I know you do. And I want it, too. Our relationship can't go on like this."

"Relationship?"

"Whatever you want to call it, there's something between us, and we have to be adults and face it. Let's meet in half an hour. What do you say?"

Please say no, please say yes, I don't exactly know what I'm asking of you . . .

"Half an hour? Okay."

My God—is he actually agreeing to this?

"Good. I'll send you an address."

"All right."

Look, man, at least ask me whose address!

"I sent it. Did you get it?"

"Yes, I got it."

"I'll see you there in half an hour."

Khaa'ina threw her phone down on the couch without a word. Qaa'id patted her shoulder, Khaa'in and Mutarjima seated on the couch. They had all heard the conversation, which Khaa'ina had put on speakerphone. "He agreed. He knew all about my involvement in what happened, and still he agreed to come. I can't believe it."

Khaa'in moved closer to her. "Believe it," he said. "You could have asked him to kill his grandfather for your sake, and he'd have done it. I've never been consumed by an infatuation before, but I've heard stories, and this is one of them."

Throwing him a look of disgust, Khaa'ina stood up. She asked whether they were ready, and they said they were. Qaa'id tried to talk about something else, but Khaa'ina silenced him. "I don't want to hear it, if you don't mind. Let's get this thing over with, and then go our separate ways."

Tension and worry could be read in Mutarjima's face. She would carry double the responsibility borne by the others since the operation was to be carried out in her home. She had been surprised by her own consent to having her place serve as the stage, but Khaa'ina's words yesterday, and her extraordinary self-confidence, had left Mutarjima no avenue for retreat.

After fifteen minutes, Khaa'ina's phone rang.

"What's the apartment number?"

"Third floor, apartment nine."

The three coconspirators hid in the bedroom, as they had agreed, reminding Khaa'ina as they went that the grandson must sit with his back to them, so that they could sneak up on him. The doorbell rang. At the door, Khaa'ina extended her hand in greeting. He seized it, pulled her to him, and embraced her. With mixed feelings, she reciprocated. Placing her hands on his cheeks, she moved his face back from hers a little to look at him. Their eyes met.

"Why are you in love with me? How can you fall in love with a woman you've seen only once?"

He didn't answer. He didn't say anything at all. He stood still and fixed her in his searching gaze, his eyes taking her in entirely, up and down. Then he brought his face close to hers and kissed her. He wound one hand into her hair, encircling her waist with the other arm, locking her lips to his. She had not in the least expected a scene like this. Peeking out from their hiding place, the other three felt like extras on a movie set. Still locked in an embrace, Khaa'ina and the grandson moved toward the couch; their witnesses could hear them breathing. Khaa'ina found it mortifying that her colleagues were watching her, but her pleasure exceeded her embarrassment. A moment later, the grandson slipped his hand under her shirt, but she stopped him. He tried again, but she grabbed his hand roughly and thrust it away from her with a force he hadn't expected. For a moment he was thrown. He had come to meet her wanting to smack her for what she'd done, but on seeing her he'd understood his own helplessness in her presence. He closed the distance between them again and took her hand.

"What is it you want?" he said. "Why did you call me?"

"Sit down and let's talk."

"Why are you so hard to read? I can't figure you out."

"What do you want to know?"

"I don't want to know anything. I just want you to stay with me—that's all. I want to see you always."

"And your grandfather?"

"You're not in competition with my grandfather. Don't be naïve."

"Your being here now, with everything that you know, means your stupidity knows no bounds . . . or you're so hopelessly lovesick you can't think straight. I hope it's the first one."

He moved in to kiss her again. She tried to push him away, but this time she couldn't. It seemed to her things were getting out of hand. "Sit down—I want to talk to you." He didn't hear her. It was as if he was inhaling her—her face, her eyes, her hair, even the sound of her voice.

"Sit down." No use. "Sit down, sit down." He held her with a feeble strength, further sapped by his adoration of her. She felt beset by contradictions. She was sure that, if he kept this up for one more minute, kissing her and breathing in the scent of her, her plan would collapse utterly. With this in mind, she steeled her resolve and wriggled free of his grasp. She backed up to sit in a chair facing the room in which her friends were hiding. This was her cue to the grandson to sit on the couch opposite her. At last he did as he was told. He leaned back, his eyes fastened on her. Everything he was about to say to her was meaningless. The only reality for him was that he was out of his depth, helpless with a passion from which he had no idea how to free himself, even as he was denied all pleasure in it. It occurred to him he might question her about Friday and her phone call to him, but he immediately rejected this thought. What would he gain by asking? Would he stand up and walk out on her for having so despicably conspired against him? He was with her now, he'd held her in his arms, and he'd felt from her some measure of desire for him. What more did he want?

"Would you like something to drink?"

"No."

"I'm going to have something. I'll make you some coffee."

"Fine."

She stood up, hoping it would all be over quickly. She didn't want to be looking at him when her wretched colleagues—caught in this tragedy of errors none of them wanted but all of them had made—crept up behind him for the attack. She heard him ask her whose home this was. She heard him ask her what she was going to do now that she had resigned. She heard him mumble. She heard his voice fade. She heard him gasp. She turned, and saw him laid out on the couch, Khaa'in pressing the chloroform pad against his nose.

The four of them saw in one another's eyes the shared knowledge that, in a matter of seconds, they had morphed from journalists to criminals. Mutarjima produced the heavy rope she'd bought the day before and helped Khaa'in get the grandson positioned on a chair. She and Qaa'id secured him to the back of the chair. They gagged and blindfolded him.

Declaring that she'd played out her own role, Khaa'ina asked them to be quick about executing the next step. Qaa'id took out his phone, and asked who was going to call the eldest son.

"You are, naturally."

They gathered around Qaa'id as he placed the call and put it on speaker.

"Hello?"

"Hello."

"Hi."

"You don't recognize my voice? Good. I—"

"You again? Do you idiots never learn?"

"You'll know who the idiot is in just a minute. Listen, you prick, we've got your son now. You and your senile father have twenty-four hours. If the old man doesn't give us his account of the *Nakba* within that time, we'll leave your son where the dogs will eat him before anyone finds him. Twenty-four hours—that's it. The old man's memories in exchange for your son's life. Any attempt on your part to contact the police and your son's life is forfeit. Understand? Twenty-four hours. Our demands must be met by nine o'clock tomorrow morning. Otherwise, you can say goodbye to your boy."

Qaa'id ended the call and looked at his colleagues. The eldest son tried to call back, but Qaa'id didn't pick up. He turned again to the others and cried, "Turn off your phones!"

They had made minute preparations for what would happen next. They'd bought plenty of chloroform and they'd agreed that they would apply the pad three or four times over the coming twenty-four hours. They would allow the grandson to eat, but not to use the bathroom. They would all stay in Mutarjima's apartment until the deadline. The grandson could be no trouble to them, the chloroform being strong enough to subdue him, even while it would do him no permanent harm. All at once Mutarjima remembered Abir. Did Abir know, she asked Khaa'in, where he lived, or where any of his relatives lived? He said no. "He's going to call her," said Mutarjima. "That's where the danger lies."

She was right. After two hours of nonstop calls to all his son's friends and colleagues, as well as a visit to his workplace, the eldest son understood that this was not just some nasty prank, and that his son had indeed been kidnapped. The sight of his son's car in the parking lot at work made things still more puzzling. How had they managed to lure him? What sort of fool would go to see them after all that had happened? Then he thought of Abir. He called her and told her everything. Her sharp intake of breath told him she wasn't lying when she swore that she had known nothing of the plot. He begged her to tell him where one of them, any of them, lived, and she swore again that she didn't know.

"Are they actually criminals?" he said to her. "Are they capable of hurting him?"

"This is frightening. How can it have come to kidnapping and threats? Give them what they want—please!"

"They've kidnapped my son, Abir. Do you know what that means?"

"Don't call the police. Please don't escalate matters. I'll try to reach them."

"It's no good. Their phones are turned off."

"Go and tell your father."

"He'll pass out from shock."

"There's no alternative. He's the only one who can put an end to this mess. I don't want to give the impression that I'm defending them, but they lost their jobs and their reputations, and now they've got a grudge against you. Please—put an end to this thing safely."

By about noon, the four conspirators were expecting the grandson to regain consciousness at any moment. Qaa'id, Mutarjima, and Khaa'in wondered whether the blindfold and gag should be removed. They were surprised by Khaa'ina's response: "No," she said, "don't take them off. I don't want him to see me. I wouldn't be able to bear the look in his eyes or the sound of his voice—I might just shoot you all and rescue him. No more emotional confrontations. Let's keep it serious and professional, and just get this thing over with."

The grandson woke up less than half an hour later. He tried to move his limbs but had no luck. He was aware of his predicament, but he didn't entirely understand what had happened to him. Khaa'in approached him. "Listen, you son of a bitch," he said. "We've got you now, and struggling will get you nowhere. We called your father and gave him twenty-four hours. If your grandfather doesn't give us his account of the *Nakba*, we'll make another *nakba* out of you. Understand?" The grandson stopped squirming and went still. His four captors waited for some further reaction from him, but there was none. Khaa'ina wished she could see into him at that moment and read his thoughts. Khaa'in explained that the grandson could request food by jiggling the chair a bit, but they would not allow him to speak or to see them or to move around for any reason.

The eldest son headed home in his car. There were moments when he was on the point of calling the police, but he wondered what he would say to them. *Four reporters kidnapped my son in order to force my father to produce his memories of the Palestinian* Nakba. Who would believe such a story? He'd be exposing himself and his father to an unend-ing stream of interrogations. What was this nightmare he was living through? *This is what your silence has come to, Papa.* There were crimes of passion, crimes of honor, and crimes having to do with money, but now he was up against a crime of memory. *Congratulations, Papa—you've added a new kind of crime for people to fear.* He got home and thought over how to break the news to his father. He saw him in his room, where he was lying down. He went and greeted him.

"Why are you home early?"

"Something's happened, Papa. It's bad."

"God forbid—what is it?"

"It's those bastards, Papa. They've kidnapped him, Papa." The eldest son crumpled as he delivered the news. "They took your grandson, Papa. They kidnapped him."

"Who kidnapped him? What are you talking about?"

"The reporters. They took him this morning and gave us twenty-four hours. If you don't turn over your account of the *Nakba* to them by nine o'clock tomorrow morning, they're going to hurt him."

The old man was silent.

"Please, Papa. Please, have mercy on me and on him—on all of us. Lift this curse. Give them what they want, Papa. Give them what they want."

"Go away and leave me alone."

"Papa . . ."

"Go away, and shut the door."

The eldest son went out, leaving his father alone. The old man got up from the bed and went to the closet. He took something out, put it on the table, and sat down. He rested his head on the back of the chair, brooding on the state of affairs in which he found himself. They wanted his memories of the *Nakba*. Which *Nakba*, exactly? Should he explain to them just how many *Nakbas* he'd been through in his life? Every day that had passed since he left his village had been a *Nakba*. *You want information, you want stories you motherfuckers? What will you do with them? Will you publish them in a book, or put them in a museum for people to gawk at, wringing their hands and feeling so very sorry? Memories.* The only word that could ever enrage him more was "Israel." *Memories.* "What happened to you?" He'd heard this question as a youth, as a bachelor, when he got married, as a father, as a grand-father, as a working man, as a retiree, in strength and in infirmity. "What happened to you? What happened to you?"

The eldest son put his ear to his father's bedroom door. He heard him muttering but couldn't make out any words. He tried to call the reporters, but their phones were still turned off. An hour later, the old man came out of his room. He looked at his son, and for a moment he hated him.

"Did you talk to them?"

"Their phones are turned off."

"What they're after—it's done."

"What do you mean?"

"My memories. I've prepared them."

"I don't understand—what do you mean 'prepared them'?"

"Come and I'll give you a notebook."

"Have you been writing down your recollections in a notebook all these years?"

"It doesn't matter. You don't need to know. When they call you, tell them what they want is ready."

"No, it does matter—it matters, Papa. You've been writing down your memories and hiding them from me?"

"See that? You're just like them. You're no different."

"Papa, wait. I'm trying to understand. Where are your . . . your memoirs?"

"They're not for you. Just go and free my grandson from them."

"What about me, Papa? How can you let them read the account before I do?"

"Kidnap me, or kidnap your son, and then demand memories in exchange for our freedom."

The old man's words were full of scorn. He went back into his room and slammed the door. The eldest son got up and paced, back and forth, back and forth, agitated, wringing his hands, sighing, cursing Israel, his life, his past, and all the causes of sorrows that had come down upon his unfortunate family. He tried calling the group again, tried ten times, but it was no use. He left the house, was gone for some hours, and when he came back nothing had changed. His father had kept a journal? He couldn't believe it. What was the old man going to give them? He had expected his father to propose that the reporters be asked to the house with the understanding that he would allow an interview and make a statement, as they wished—but for him to give them something in writing? He checked his phone again. An hour passed, and then another, and another, and night fell. Exactly at midnight, his phone rang.

"WHY DID YOU TURN OFF YOUR PHONES, YOU DOGS? Where is my son? Is he all right?"

"One more word and you'll hear him braying like the ass he is. Quit yapping and tell us what's going on with you."

"Not until I know he's unharmed."

"It seems you don't get it. Your son is at our mercy. If you piss us off any more, you'll hear him scream. I promise you that."

"What you're demanding is here."

"What do you mean?"

"My father has kept a journal—everything's in a notebook. It's yours as soon as you set my son free."

"How are we to be sure what's in the notebook is really his recollections? Couldn't you have bought a notebook and filled it up with nonsense of your own invention?"

"My father said he would give you a notebook containing his memories. That's all I have. I have no other guarantees. I had no idea, by the way, that he kept a journal. Let's finish this business—fast."

"We need some guarantee that you and your son won't go to the police."

"We won't. I swear to you, I won't. Let's conduct ourselves like adults and meet somewhere. I give you the notebook, you give me my son."

Khaa'in had put the phone on speaker, so the grandson heard the conversation. The four conspirators all perceived that the chair to which the grandson was tied shifted a little when the eldest son mentioned that the old man would give them his journal, and a few moments later tears began to run down the grandson's cheeks, flowing from beneath his blindfold. Unable to bear this sight, Khaa'ina ran to him to remove the blindfold, but Qaa'id stopped her. As the grandson struggled to articulate something, it seemed as though he would choke on the gag. Khaa'in glanced at Qaa'id, his eyebrows raised quizzically. Qaa'id gestured to let things be, not wishing to allow the grandson to influence anyone by speaking at such an emotional moment. The grandson mumbled some more, and his chair shuddered again as he tried to stand up. Khaa'in went over to him. "Listen," he warned, "we've done you no bodily harm up to now, but we could beat you for hours, and avenge ourselves for what you did to us on Friday. Settle down. It's all over." But the grandson did not settle down. For a full half hour he struggled, until his strength gave out, and he exhaled painfully. His tears subsided, then began again, evidently his only means now of expressing the pain he was in. *Don't do it, Grandpa. Don't give them your memories, Grandpa. They won't dare do anything to me. No, you won't, you sons of bitches. I'm the cause of all this, Grandpa, goddamn it all—my grandfather, my grandfather, no one gets near your memories, beloved Grandfather, you were my source of comfort . . . Let me go, you sons of bitches and then you'll see . . . No, Grandpa, no no no, your one wish for the rest of your life was that you be allowed to keep your memories to yourself—please, Grandpa, please . . . you motherfuckers, no, no . . .*

Khaa'in called the eldest son again. "We'll send you an address," he said. "Come alone and bring the notebook. Don't try any funny business."

Khaa'in gestured to Khaa'ina to join him, leaving Qaa'id and Mutarjima alone with the grandson. They went to the corner of Mutarjima's street and sent the address to the eldest son via WhatsApp. The eldest son was there within fifteen minutes. He looked at them from his car window. His father had enjoined him when he handed over the notebook not to open it. "Swear an oath," he told him, and the eldest son had done so. It amazed him to find that he did not renege on his promise. He'd placed the notebook on the passenger seat and merely glanced at it now and then as he drove. The *Nakba,* his son kidnapped, the old man, the memories, fifty years—opening the notebook would bridge the gap . . . and yet he didn't do it. He had mixed feelings, the notebook sitting there beside him, and yet he didn't do it. The past, his father's history, stories he'd dreamed for decades of hearing, and yet he refrained.

The eldest son got out of his car, and Khaa'in stepped forward, beckoning to him to come closer. He searched him thoroughly, making sure he wasn't carrying anything like a weapon, then went with him to the car. It was two o'clock in the morning, and there was no one about. The eldest son sat in the back seat, between Khaa'in and Khaa'ina.

"Where's the notebook?"

"In the briefcase."

"Unlock the briefcase."

"No. Not until you let him go."

"Oh, well, then we have no choice but to blindfold you and tie you up until we arrive."

Khaa'ina got into the driver's seat while Khaa'in stayed next to the eldest son. They set off for Mutarjima's building. None of them said a word.

They maneuvered the eldest son inside, positioning him in front of the grandson. Qaa'id came forward. "Now we'll let you see each other, but don't do anything stupid. Remember, we could beat the crap out of you both, but we won't let it come to that. Once you've seen that your son is unharmed, turn over the notebook to us. Then we'll release him. Agreed?"

The eldest son nodded. The grandson whimpered. The eldest son's blindfold was removed first, and his hands untied. Seeing his son before him, bound and gagged, he let out a moan. He unlocked the briefcase, took out the notebook, and showed it to them. "Here it is," he said. "Let him go, and take it." Qaa'id went to him and asked to see it, to make sure, but the eldest son held back. "Set him free first."

"We have to make sure that what's in the notebook is what we asked for."

"This is my father's notebook. I swear to you it's my father's notebook which he said contained his recollections. Release my son."

"Put it on the kitchen table."

The eldest son did as he was told, after some hesitation. Khaa'in escorted him to the kitchen table, where the notebook was placed, then accompanied him back and seated him before his son. Khaa'ina ran into the bedroom, closing the door behind her; the eldest son understood nothing of this. Positioned on either side of the grandson, Khaa'in and Qaa'id untied him and tried to help him to his feet, but he couldn't stand up. When they removed the blindfold and the gag, he looked quickly around for her, not finding her. His father embraced him, weeping. Qaa'id took out a pistol and aimed it at them.

"Get out—now—and don't make any sudden moves."

"Put down the gun—we're going. There's no need for all that."

The grandson rubbed his eyes and scanned the living room. She must be somewhere in the apartment. He'd heard her voice more than once while he was tied up—she couldn't have vanished in an instant, just like that. His father took him by the hand. "Let's go," he said, but the grandson stood rooted in place, searching everywhere with his eyes. When he caught sight of the notebook on the kitchen table, he scowled, muttering, "Sons of bitches, sons of bitches . . ." Losing his temper, Khaa'in advanced, but Qaa'id restrained him.

"Get out of here, while you still can. Take your son and go."

Still the grandson stood, staring at the bedroom door. In that moment his father realized what he was looking for, and part of the story began to come together for him. He embraced his son and headed for the door of the apartment. On the threshold he turned as if he had just remembered something.

"Are you going to open the notebook?"

"That's no concern of yours. Now go."

Qaa'id was still aiming his weapon at them.

"Open it and read it in our presence."

"No. We're done here."

"But *we'll* never be done. We'll never be done," the eldest son said in a strangled voice, his face flushed.

"What is it you want, exactly? I don't understand."

"Nothing. We're going."

Through the open door the father and son went, turning their backs on the rest. Hearing the sound of the front door opening, Khaa'ina emerged from the bedroom, and stopped in the doorway. The grandson turned and their eyes met. No one spoke. It was as if everyone was waiting for some momentous occurrence. Khaa'ina wished the grandson would hurry up and go. The grandson wished Khaa'ina would run to him. She realized that if in this moment he confessed his love for her, she would not let him leave—she would tear up the notebook and fling the fragments in her colleagues' faces. The grandson realized that if she asked him to stay, he would stay, even if it meant being gunned down. She knew she did not love him, but she craved his lust for her; he knew he was incapable of hating her. The father patted his son's shoulder. "Let's go," he said.

When they were gone, Khaa'ina had to fight back the urge to cry. She moved toward the notebook, but Mutarjima got there first. The others came forward and the four of them gathered in a circle. They could hardly believe that they finally had the old man in their clutches. If only that could have been the outcome of their very first meeting, none of this would have happened. A notebook, sheets of paper, memories, a *Nakba*. Why had that been so impossible for all these weeks? Mutarjima opened the notebook. They all took in the first page, on which there was just a single line.

MEMORIES OF THE *NAKBA*

Mutarjima turned to the next page. There was a date and what might have been a chapter heading or an introductory sentence:

5/15/1948
Palestine was lost.

But the rest of the page was blank. Mutarjima turned the page again.

5/15/1949
Palestine was lost.

The two pages looked identical: a date followed by "Palestine was lost," and nothing else. She turned to the next page:

5/15/1950
Palestine was lost.

Mutarjima flung the notebook aside. They all stared at one another. Khaa'ina was unsure whether to laugh until she cried or cry until she laughed. She retrieved the notebook and reopened to the page where they'd left off:

5/15/1951
Palestine was lost.

She continued now, turning the pages over slowly, occasionally glancing up at her friends.

5/15/1952
Palestine was lost.

5/15/1953
Palestine was lost.

5/15/1954
Palestine was lost.

5/15/1955
Palestine was lost.

5/15/1956
Palestine was lost.

5/15/1957
Palestine was lost.

5/15/1958
Palestine was lost.

5/15/1959
Palestine was lost.

5/15/1960
Palestine was lost.

5/15/1961
Palestine was lost.

5/15/1962
Palestine was lost.

5/15/1963
Palestine was lost.

5/15/1964
Palestine was lost.

5/15/1965
Palestine was lost.

5/15/1966
Palestine was lost.

5/15/1967
Palestine was lost.

5/15/1968
Palestine was lost.

5/15/1969
Palestine was lost.

5/15/1970
Palestine was lost.

5/15/1971
Palestine was lost.

5/15/1972
Palestine was lost.

5/15/1973
Palestine was lost.

5/15/1974
Palestine was lost.

5/15/1975
Palestine was lost.

5/15/1976
Palestine was lost.

5/15/1977
Palestine was lost.

5/15/1978
Palestine was lost.

5/15/1979
Palestine was lost.

5/15/1980
Palestine was lost.

5/15/1981
Palestine was lost.

5/15/1982
Palestine was lost.

5/15/1983
Palestine was lost.

5/15/1984
Palestine was lost.

5/15/1985
Palestine was lost.

5/15/1986
Palestine was lost.

5/15/1987
Palestine was lost.

5/15/1988
Palestine was lost.

5/15/1989
Palestine was lost.

5/15/1990
Palestine was lost.

5/15/1991
Palestine was lost.

5/15/1992
Palestine was lost.

5/15/1993
Palestine was lost.

5/15/1994
Palestine was lost.

5/15/1995
Palestine was lost.

5/15/1996
Palestine was lost.

5/15/1997
Palestine was lost.

5/15/1998
Palestine was lost.

5/15/1999
Palestine was lost.

5/15/2000
Palestine was lost.

5/15/2001
Palestine was lost.

5/15/2002
Palestine was lost.

5/15/2003
Palestine was lost.

5/15/2004
Palestine was lost.

5/15/2005
Palestine was lost.

5/15/2006
Palestine was lost.

5/15/2007
Palestine was lost.

5/15/2008
Palestine was lost.

5/15/2009
Palestine was lost.

5/15/2010
Palestine was lost.

5/15/2011
Palestine was lost.

5/15/2012
Palestine was lost.

5/15/2013
Palestine was lost.

5/15/2014
Palestine was lost.

5/15/2015
Palestine was lost.

5/15/2016
Palestine was lost.

5/15/2017
Palestine was lost.

5/15/2018
Palestine was lost.

None of the journalists had any further desire to comment on what they'd read. They gathered up their belongings and stood in the center of the room. A sense of loss engulfed them, a feeling that they would never see each other again after this, and that their yearslong friendship had been demolished at the hands of the old man. One by one they headed for the door. Mutarjima sat immobile on the living-room couch, as if only waiting for them to be gone. Just as Khaa'ina reached the door, Mutarjima jumped up and, catching her at the threshold, seized her hand. "Didn't I tell you?" she whispered. "We all lost everything—all except you. You got the consolation prize."

Amman – Doha, 2019

Acknowledgments

Immense thanks to Omar Khalifah for giving me the honor of translating his first novel into English–can't wait to see your next work of fiction, Omar!

My gratitude as well to Jeremy Davies, first of all for loving this book and wanting to help bring the English rendition into print, and then for working so intensively toward that end.

Collaborating with both of you has been a pleasure!

Coffee House Press began as a small letterpress operation in 1972 and has grown into an internationally renowned nonprofit publisher of literary fiction, essay, poetry, and other work that doesn't fit neatly into genre categories.

Coffee House is both a publisher and an arts organization. Through our *Books in Action* program and publications, we've become interdisciplinary collaborators and incubators for new work and audience experiences. Our vision for the future is one where a publisher is a catalyst and connector.

LITERATURE
is not the same thing as
PUBLISHING

Funder Acknowledgments

Coffee House Press is an internationally renowned independent book publisher and arts nonprofit based in Minneapolis, MN; through its literary publications and *Books in Action* program, Coffee House acts as a catalyst and connector—between authors and readers, ideas and resources, creativity and community, inspiration and action.

Coffee House Press books are made possible through the generous support of grants and donations from corporations, state and federal grant programs, family foundations, and the many individuals who believe in the transformational power of literature. This activity is made possible by the voters of Minnesota through a Minnesota State Arts Board Operating Support grant, thanks to the legislative appropriation from the Arts and Cultural Heritage Fund. Coffee House also receives major operating support from the Amazon Literary Partnership, Jerome Foundation, Literary Arts Emergency Fund, McKnight Foundation, and the National Endowment for the Arts (NEA). To find out more about how NEA grants impact individuals and communities, visit www.arts.gov.

Coffee House Press receives additional support from Bookmobile; the Buckley Charitable Fund; Dorsey & Whitney LLP; the Gaea Foundation; the Schwab Charitable Fund; and the U.S. Bank Foundation.

The Publisher's Circle of Coffee House Press

Publisher's Circle members make significant contributions to Coffee House Press's annual giving campaign. Understanding that a strong financial base is necessary for the press to meet the challenges and opportunities that arise each year, this group plays a crucial part in the success of Coffee House's mission.

Recent Publisher's Circle members include many anonymous donors, Patricia A. Beithon, Theodore Cornwell, Jane Dalrymple-Hollo, Mary Ebert and Paul Stembler, Kamilah Foreman, Eva Galiber, Roger Hale and Nor Hall, William Hardacker, Randy Hartten and Ron Lotz, Carl and Heidi Horsch, Amy L. Hubbard and Geoffrey J. Kehoe Fund of the St. Paul & Minnesota Foundation, Hyde Family Charitable Fund, Kenneth & Susan Kahn, the Kenneth Koch Literary Estate, Cinda Kornblum, the Lenfestey Family Foundation, Carol and Aaron Mack, Gillian McCain, Mary and Malcolm McDermid, Daniel N. Smith III and Maureen Millea Smith, Vance Opperman, Mr. Pancks' Fund in memory of Graham Kimpton, Alan Polsky, Robin Preble, Ronald Restrepo and Candace S. Baggett, Steve Smith, Jeffrey Sugerman and Sarah Schultz, Paul Thissen, Grant Wood, Margaret Wurtele, Jeremy M. Davies, Robin Chemers Neustein, Dorsey and Whitney Foundation, The Buckley Charitable Fund, Elizabeth Schnieders, Allyson Tucker, and Aptara Inc.

For more information about the Publisher's Circle and other ways to support Coffee House Press books, authors, and activities, please visit www.coffeehousepress.org/pages/donate or contact us at info@coffeehousepress.org.

Omar Khalifah is a Palestinian writer and academic. His book, *Nasser in the Egyptian Imaginary,* was published in English by Edinburgh University Press in 2017. His collection *Ka'annani Ana* (As If I Were Myself) was published in Amman, Jordan, in 2010, and his novel *Qabid al-Raml* (Sand-Catcher) was published in 2020. His articles have appeared in *Middle East Critique* and *Journal of World Literature.* A Fulbright scholar, Khalifah is an associate professor of Arabic Literature and Culture at Georgetown School of Foreign Service in Qatar.

Barbara Romaine is an academic and literary translator. She has published translations of six novels, most recently *Waiting for the Past* (Syracuse University Press, 2022), by the Iraqi novelist Hadiya Hussein. She has held two NEA fellowships in translation, one of which was for her work on Radwa Ashour's *Spectres* (Interlink Books, 2011). *Spectres* went on to place second in the 2011 Saif Ghobash-Banipal international translation competition. Romaine's translations of essays, short stories, and classical poetry have appeared in a variety of literary periodicals.

Sand-Catcher was designed by
Bookmobile Design & Digital Publisher Services.
Text is set in Minion Pro.